Someday This Will Be Funny

Someday This Will Be Funny

Lynne Tillman

Red Lemonade

a Cursor publishing community

Brooklyn, New York

2011

Library of Congress Control Number 2010941274
ISBN 978-1-935869-00-9

Cover design by Charles Orr
Interior design by Fogelson-Lubliner
Printed in the United States of America

Red Lemonade
a Cursor publishing community
Brooklyn, New York

www.redlemona.de

Distributed by Publishers Group West

10 9 8 7 6 5 4 3 2 1

Table of Contents

I   That's How Wrong My Love Is

9   The Unconscious is Also Ridiculous

11   The Substitute

19   Chartreuse

25   A Simple Idea

31   Give Us Some Dirt

35   Playing Hurt

43   More Sex

47   Dear Ollie

51   But There's A Family Resemblance

61   The Original Impulse

71   The Shadow of a Doubt

83   Lunacies

87   The Way We Are

91   A Greek Story

95   The Recipe

107   Later

111   Love Sentence

137   Impressions of an Artist, with Haiku

143   Madame Realism's Conscience

153   Save Me from the Pious and the Vengeful

For Harry Mathews

That's How Wrong My Love Is

A while back, I watched a pair of mourning doves in their nest every day, watched as one then the other sat on an egg; saw their baby emerge from the egg, watched its being carried food and fed, saw them all fly away one late summer morning, never to return, I thought. But there are many mourning doves around my neighborhood and maybe those three are back.

Every morning, right to the window; every afternoon, come home, open the door, right to the window—I witnessed the entire cycle of a nesting mother and father, a chick's beak cracking through the eggshell, the baby's care, its parents' nurturing it, the baby's first flight.

The mother and father took turns sitting on the egg, and I was informed by a genuine birder, a nature writer, that this behavior was unexpected and unusual. One bird sits, the other flies away and returns with food, the sitter flies off, then the food gatherer guards the egg, mother and father switching roles to protect the egg, that was unusual, I was told.

The nest rested in an empty planter on a windowsill on another building directly across from my window; I strained to see it, a city backyard away. I thought about getting a telescope, but in the city—

remember *Rear Window*—that can be dangerous or at least provocative. I would have to train my sights carefully and somehow declare my looking benign, when most looking is not. As far as I know there is no gesture, like waving a white flag, to signify a lack of aggression in looking. As for the people whose window it was, and whose planter it was, I never met them, or saw them at the small window, and I often wondered how they felt about the avian family on their ledge. After the birds left, the planter was quickly filled with flowers, so I understood that they disliked the birds' nesting at their window. I disliked them for that, since mourning doves are supposed to return to their nests, and now they couldn't. This might sound strange to non-New Yorkers, but many backyards of smaller apartment buildings are quiet, untrafficked, almost bucolic settings. It's quiet and calm behind many buildings, which are not in midtown, and perfect for birds.

I read about mourning doves' habits and that the males have red streaks on their necks, while the females don't; still, I couldn't tell one sex from the other. Rising in the morning and rushing to the window, cup of tea in hand, I'd make sounds I hoped they'd associate with me, friendly noises, but I was never certain that they were, or if they might be inimical in their language. I was sure, though, they noticed when I whistled or cooed.

Mourning doves have a distinctive call, a melancholy coo, melodic and even hypnotic. Curiously, the voice doesn't seem to come from them, their beaks don't look open. But if you get close enough to them, you'll notice that the feathers on the necks fluff out, and their little chests puff out and vibrate. A dove's coo is in the lower range, there are usually four or five calls in a row, sweetly mournful, though what they are mourning can only be supposed. I like their sound, though if they carried on day and night, I'd go crazy.

The reason I imagine they looked at me or in my direction, though what image they saw is a mystery, was confirmed on a special, sad morning. As usual, I made myself a cup of tea, and, cup in hand, went to the window to see the birds and the nest. They weren't there. The nest was empty. It was terrible. I gave my cry and whistled, and immediately I heard a rustling noise. I looked to my left, and there were the three birds, sitting on the bough of a big, New York weed tree.

This is what happened: I whistled again, the three gazed at me, now closer in proximity than they'd ever been, the baby half the size of its parents, so slim and sleek, and with their heads turned in my direction, there was a long moment during which we continued to look at each other. Then, suddenly, but in unison, they flew away. They'd waited for me to come to the window, they'd wanted me to know they were abandoning their nest. And me, perhaps.

I realize this sounds corny, ridiculous, or just another piece of anthropomorphism, or vanity, if feeling appreciated or recognized by birds is vanity. Yet I believe it was their intention, though I have since learned that mourning doves lack cunning and are not bright.

Not long ago, I saw a documentary about many varieties of migratory birds—*Migration*—who fly thousands of miles twice a year for food and a safe place to nest, raise their chicks, and return when the elements change; their lives are full of duress and hard work. They have little rest. While the airplane with the cinematographers flew beside the flock, the birds ignored it and singlemindedly moved forward, their wings beating rhythmically and constantly, though occasionally they glided, and they might have been exhausted; yet they kept going, determined to eat, to nest, to procreate. While the film's angles were gorgeous, and I did feel as if I were in the sky beside the birds, I had the beginnings of vertigo and was disturbed almost all the way through. I thought, their travails necessitated small, light brains; otherwise, with heavier, big brains, how could they manage flight and why would they go on living like that? If they could think, they might think, as many humans do, *life is meaningless if all I do is fly back and forth.*

The next spring, with the planter full of flowers, no birds nested across the backyard. But one day, I don't remember when, a mourning dove appeared on the fire escape at the front of our apartment, four stories up. I wondered if it was one of the three. I bought birdseed and began putting it out on the window ledge. I made the whistling and cooing sounds I did for the first family, and that bird or another and others began showing up. I also hung a birdseed feeder for finches, and they came within a week, but with five or six on the feeder, the feeder shook so much, the seed landed on the sidewalk, and hundreds of pigeons took up residence and shitted all over it. I love finches, their brilliant and subtle coloring, their tiny rounded chests, but I had to remove the feeder, or become another character on the block who caused a nuisance.

In my building there is a young woman who cannot throw out anything; she appears normal, whatever that is, but if you went into her apartment, which I was forced to do one day, to search for my absent-minded, runaway cat, Louis, the madness of her place—moth-eaten, worm-ridden, filthy rugs piled high upon a moldy couch, nearly to the ceiling; a sole, scraggly path through the apartment, between boxes and mounds of junk, probably teeming with vermin; shelves and lamps leaning against other furniture, so if one object was moved, everything would fall down—this chaos describes a very different person from the bubbly young woman who zips happily around the neighborhood. Inside her apartment that one time, I recognized some of the pieces I had thrown out years ago. She's a hoarder, a photographer, who shoots me when I don't know she's there, gleefully catching me unaware, and also a fire hazard but none of us tenants would dare tell her to examine or change her ways. Occasionally I see her daintily dropping a tiny bundle of trash into the building's garbage can.

I've been leaving seed on the ledge for about five years, and there are mourning doves who appear every day at the same time, morning and late afternoon, but I've given up trying to distinguish one from the other. Sometimes I think I can recognize them by their intelligence, but I can't really. I signal, and one, two, or three might fly to the fire escape and watch as I shovel out the seed. Some are not afraid anymore; I think they're the smart ones, they move closer to the ledge, to the seed. Some show fear and fly off; the dumb ones, even if they stay, never touch the food, even when they see it, and then many pigeons—mourning doves are in their family but pigeons are ugly and twice their size—congregate and greedily consume all of the seed.

There is nothing I can do, I have tried various methods. The smarter mourning doves recognize that, when I open the window and wave my hand in the air to shoo the pigeons, I am not shooing them away, because they remain on the fire escape and wait to eat. Yet, even after having waited, they might not go to the birdseed—again, a mystifying mix of smart and stupid. Some always do, the ones I think are smart, and then they get it before the pigeons swarm.

The mourning doves have become habituated to being fed at my window, and I have made feeding them a habit. They are dependent upon me, to some extent. I should put seed out every day, because they expect it. If I forget, they boldly approach the window and push their heads through the window gates, when the window is open, or if the window is closed, they stare into the apartment, patiently, or tap their beaks on the glass and look inside. It's odd, but they know where I live. Sometimes I leave town, and, if I remember that I'm not doing my duty to them, I feel a little guilty. Then I tell myself there is food everywhere on the streets of New York, there's a park down the block... When I return, I continue the habit.

By now the mourning doves may have learned that I am erratic or inconsistent, and maybe they don't wholly depend on me, but think of my window as a candy store, where they get treats, not real meals. But I do feel burdened with a responsibility I didn't predict when hoping to see them again.

Still, there are daily and surprising pleasures. I have seen them have sex. Mourning doves mate for life, I've been told, and they're tender with each other before and after sex. The seduction begins when the female grooms or teases the male—I can tell male from female only then, because side by side the female is much smaller. The female pokes and ruffles the feathers of her mate, and, after a while, they face each other and kiss. They kiss a few times, open beaked, then the male mounts the female, there's a brief spasm or shudder, and the male alights, he again sits next to the female, they nuzzle and face each other, and then kiss a few more times. This behavior is not an anomaly, all of the mourning doves who have had sex on my fire escape follow the same ritual.

I love animals, I am an animal, I'm a mammal, a human being, I like most people, love many, despise one person, though I don't want to hate anyone. I am also selfish and want what I want. My greatest and most enduring problems in life are ethical, but living ethically is necessarily a conscious endeavor, the unconscious is not ethical, and questions and riddles about correct behavior are endless in variation, new issues coming along all the time—stalking on the Internet, for example. Not feeding the mourning doves regularly is wrong, but I generally give myself a pass. My not feeding the pigeons because I find them big and ugly is unethical. A self-named animal lover should feed all creatures alike. Worse, I am not a vegetarian. I love animals but discriminate among them and eat some. I eat less meat than I once did. I like steak, but usually resist it—for my health more than for the cow's; I rarely resist roast chicken. I don't eat bacon, I eat fish, crustaceans, but I would never eat horse, cat, or dog.

If I were starving, caught in a war, desperate to survive, like the Donner Party who ate their dead colleagues, like most people, ultimately I would succumb, with remorse and disgust.

I hope to do no harm, yet I cause harm, about which I may have no knowledge, which is a dilemma I don't expect will change or that I can entirely overcome: the predicament between principle and desire. There are things I like to do, and I do them, and, as much as I can, I don't do what I don't want to do.

The Unconscious is Also Ridiculous

One, she can jump very high, leap over subway turnstiles, she can rise and fly over stairs or over crowds anywhere. She can fly up flights of stairs, with no effort, and land wherever she wants, gracefully, weightlessly. She can do this whenever she wants. This is her secret gift, but she is cautious and does not use it.

Two, she is an amazing short-distance runner. Her high school gym teacher watches her, during a baseball game, run to first base, clocks her speed, and selects her to compete in the 100-yard dash. She stays for practice every day after class. Her heart beats wildly in her young chest as she plants her shoe at the starting line and the gun goes off. She runs as if the devil is chasing her. Her legs carry her so fast, she's in the air, galloping. Her high school record is never defeated.

Three, she is a tennis player, a great champion in her prime. At the age of eight, her tennis chops were recognized, and her parents sent her to tennis camp. She had great instructors, who encouraged her, and her parents became her biggest fans and enthusiasts. They did everything they could to let her play tennis. They moved to a warm climate. They found her tutors and the best coaches, former pros. Her main coach thought she could win the U.S. Open, if she kept her head down and fought for it. By thirteen, she was in the juniors, winning trophy after trophy. She liked winning. When she was down two or three games, she came back. When she was down a set, she came back. She had no fear of failure, she took the court confidently. She didn't worry that her friends would hate her for being better at tennis than they were. She was a competitor.

Her life was as simple as the lines on a tennis court.

The fantasy ends there, always.

Actually, she thinks that life as a pro would become monotonous and grim. That she could not hit the ball and practice her serve hour after hour, day after day. She thinks the women on the tour are tougher than she could ever be, and she doesn't know what she'd talk about with them, after tennis. She avoids the sun, and believes sun screen is futile when sweating. She'd worry about skin cancer and other injuries. Mostly, she thinks she'd go crazy playing all the time. And, Andre Agassi's recent confession that he hated playing tennis, that every match was torture for him, has devastated her. She loves, loved, Agassi.

No matter. She maintains the belief that, if her parents had recognized her gift and gotten her a great coach, she could have won the Open, and maybe a Grand Slam. The fantasy returns every year, with the Open, Wimbledon, the French Open, and the Australian. In it, she is twelve, young and lean, her hair is pulled back from her thin, intent face. Her baseball cap shades her nose and cheeks. She is playing against two friends, two guys who can't return her serve. Her backhand is fierce.

She replays her winning games and the feeling of lifting the trophy above her head to a roaring crowd. She's crying. She wins and wins. Her life is tennis.

The Substitute

She watched his heart have a small fit under his black T-shirt. Its unsteady rhythm was a bridge between them. Lost in the possibilities he offered her, she studied his thin face, aquiline nose, tobacco-yellow fingers. In the moment, which swallowed her whole, she admired his need to smoke. She wouldn't always, but not being able to stop meant something, now. Certain damage was sexy, a few sinuous scars. He'd be willing, eager maybe, to exist with her in the margins.

She'd set the terms. Ride, nurse on danger, take acceptable or necessary risks. Maybe there'd be one night at a luscious border, where they'd thrum on thrill, ecstatically unsure, or one long day into one long night, when they'd say everything and nothing and basely have their way with each other. She wasn't primitive but had an idea of it—to live for and in her senses. She'd tell him this. Then they'd vanish, disappear without regret. She was astonished at how adolescence malingered in every cell of her mature body.

Helen met Rex on the train. She taught interior design to art students in a small college in a nearby city. He taught painting. She liked it that he sometimes smelled like a painter, which was old-fashioned, though he wasn't; he told her he erased traces of the hand (she liked hands), used acrylics, didn't leave his mark and yet left it, too. Still, tobacco, chemicals, alcohol, a certain raw body odor, all the storied ingredients, reminded her of lofts and studios and herself in them twenty years before, late at night, time dissolving.

Between Rex and her, one look established furtive interest, and with a fleeting, insubstantial communication they betrayed that and themselves. They were intrigued dogs sniffing each other's tempting genitals and asses. Being an animal contented her lately, and she sometimes compared her behavior with wild and domestic ones. Reason, she told an indignant friend with relish, was too great a price to pay daily.

Her imagination was her best feature. It embellished her visible parts, and altogether they concocted longing in Rex. She could see it; she could have him. She couldn't have her analyst. She held Dr. Kaye in her mind, where she frolicked furiously in delayed gratification. But Rex, this man beside her—she could see the hairs on his arms quiver—engaged her fantastic self, an action figure.

Rex's hands fooled with his cigarette pack. Her analyst didn't smoke, at least not with her, and she didn't imagine he smoked at home, with his wife, whose office was next door, she discovered, unwittingly, not ever having considered that the woman in the adjoining office was more than a colleague. Cottage industry, she remarked in her session. Dr. Kaye seemed amused. Maybe because she hadn't been curious about the relationship or because it took her so long to catch on. That meant more than what she said, she supposed.

Rex's hands weren't well-shaped, beautiful. If she concentrated on them… But she wondered: would they stir me, anyway. She shut her eyes. She liked talking with her eyes shut, though she couldn't see her analyst's face. Dr. Kaye wore a long tie today. It hung down over his fly and obscured the trouser pouch for his penis.

When she first saw him, she was relieved to find him avuncular, not handsome like her father. Men grew on trees, there were so many of them, they dropped to the ground and rotted, most of them. Dr. Kaye hesitated before speaking. She imagined his face darkening when she said things like that. Whatever, she said and smiled again at the ceiling. I like men. I'm just pulling your leg. She could see the bottoms of his trousers.

When she approached him on the train, Rex had a near-smirk on his lips, just because she was near. She liked his lips, they were lopsided. If he didn't speak, she could imagine his tongue. He might push for something to happen, actually, and that was exciting. Her heart sped up as Rex glanced sideways at her, from under his… liquid hazel eyes. She squirmed, happily. Hovering at the edge tantalized her. The heart did race and skip; it fibrillated, her mother had died of that. What do you feel about your mother now? Dr. Kaye asked. But aren't you my mother now?

They flirted, she and Rex, the new, new man with a dog's name. Did it matter what he looked like naked? They hadn't lied to each other. Unless by omission. But then their moments were lived by omission. Looking at him staring out the window, as if he were thinking of things other than her, she started a sentence, then let the next word slide back into her mouth like a sucking candy. Rex held his breath. She blushed. This was really too precious to consummate.

Dr. Kaye seemed involved in the idea. He had shaved closely that morning, and his aftershave came to her in tart waves. She inhaled him. She—Ms. Vaughn, to him—weighed whether she would tell him anything about Rex, a little, or everything. With Rex, she wasn't under any agreement. She measured her words for herself and for him, and she told him just enough. He was the libertine lover, Dr. Kaye the demanding one. With him, she drew out her tales, like Scheherazade.

First, Dr. Kaye, she offered, her eyes on the ceiling, it was the way he looked at me, he was gobbling me up, taking me inside him. I liked that. Why did I like that? Because I hate myself, you know that. Then she laughed. Later, she went on, I pretended I didn't see him staring at me. Then I stopped pretending. In her next session, she continued: He wanted to take my hand, because his finger fluttered over my wrist, and his unwillingness, no, inability, I don't know about will, I had a boyfriend named Will, he was impotent, did I tell you? His reluctance made me... wet. She sat up once and stared at Dr. Kaye, daring him. But he was well-trained, an obedient dog, and he listened neatly.

Rex was sloppy with heat. Their unstable hearts could be a gift to Dr. Kaye. Or a substitute, for a substitute. She trembled, bringing their story—hers—to Dr. Kaye in installments, four times a week. It was better than a good dream, whose heady vapors were similar to her ambiguous, unlived relationships. Not falling was better, she explained to Dr. Kaye; having what they wanted was ordinary and would destroy them or be nothing, not falling, not losing, not dying was better. Why do you think that? he asked. This nothing that was almost everything gave her hope. Illusion was truth in a different guise, true in another dimension. Dr. Kaye wanted to know what she felt about Rex. I don't know—we're borderline characters, she said. Liminal, like you and me.

And, she went on, her hands folded on her stomach, he and I went into the toilet... of the train ... and fooled around. She laughed. I was in a train crash once... But the toilet smelled... Like your aftershave, she thought, but didn't say. Say everything, say everything impossible.

Looking at Rex reading a book, his skin flushed, overheated in tiny red florets, Helen wondered when the romance would become misshapen. Her need could flaunt itself. She wanted that, really, and trusted to her strangeness and his eccentricity for its acceptance. Or, lust could be checked like excess baggage at the door. They'd have a cerebral affair.

But their near-accidental meetings sweetened her days and nights. They were sweeter even than chocolate melting in her mouth. Dark chocolate helped her sleep. She had a strange metabolism. How could she sleep—Rex was the latest hero who had come to save her, to fight for her. If he didn't play on her playground, with her rules, he was less safe than Dr. Kaye. But Rex was as smart, almost, as she was; he knew how to entice her. She might go further than she planned.

Dr. Kaye's couch was a deep red, nearly purple, she noted more than once. Lying on it, Helen told him she liked Rex more than him. She hoped for an unguarded response. Why is that? he asked, somberly. Because he delivers, like the pizza man—remember the one who got murdered, some boys did it. They were bored, they didn't know what to do with themselves, so they ordered a pizza and killed the guy who brought it. The poor guy. Everyone wants to be excited. Don't you? She heard Dr Kaye's weight shift in his chair. So, she went on, Rex told me I'm beautiful, amazing, and I don't believe him, and it reminded me of when Charles—that lawyer I was doing some work for—said, out of nowhere, I was, and then that his wife and baby were going away, and would I spend the week with him, and it would be over when his wife came back—we were walking in Central Park— and I said no, and I never saw him again.

One night, Rex and she took the train home together. When they arrived at Grand Central, they decided to have a drink, for the first time. The station, its ceiling a starry night sky, had been restored to its former grandeur, and Helen felt that way, too. In a commuter bar, they did MTV humpy dancing, wet-kissed, put their hands on each other, and got thrown out. Lust was messy, gaudy. Neverneverland, never was better, if she could convince Rex. How hot is cool? they repeated to each other, after their bar imbroglio.

Helen liked waiting, wanting, and being wanted more. It's all so typical, she told Dr. Kaye, and he wanted her to go on. She felt him hanging on her words. Tell me more, he said. The bar was dark, of course, crowded, Rex's eyes were smoky, and everything in him was concentrated in them, they were like headlights, he'd been in a car accident once and showed me his scar, at his neck, and then I kissed him there, and I told him about my brother's suicide, and about you, and he was jealous, he doesn't want me to talk about him, us, he thinks it'll destroy the magic, probably... stupid... it is magic... and he wanted me then, and there... But she thought: Never with Rex, never give myself, just give this to you, my doctor. She announced, suddenly: I won't squander anything anymore.

The urge to give herself was weirdly compelling, written into her like the ridiculous, implausible vows in a marriage contract. Dr. Kaye might feel differently about marriage, or other things, but he wouldn't tell her. He contained himself astutely and grew fuller, fatter. He looked larger every week. The mystery was that he was always available for their time-bound encounters, in which thwarted love was still love. It was what you did with your limits that mattered. She imagined she interested him.

Listening to her stories, Dr. Kaye encouraged her, and she felt alive. She could do with her body what she wanted, everyone knew that; the body was just a fleshy vehicle of consequences. Her mind was virtual—free, even, to make false separations. She could lie to herself, to him; she believed in what she said, whatever it was. So did he. To Dr. Kaye, there was truth in fantasy. Her half-lies and contradictions were really inconsequential to anyone but herself. He might admit that.

But the next day, on the train, Rex pressed her silently. His thin face was as sharp as a steak knife. He wouldn't give her what she wanted: he didn't look at her with greedy passion. There was a little death around the corner, waiting for her. She had to give him something, feed his fire or lose it and him.

So she would visit his studio, see his work, she might succumb, Helen informed her analyst. She described how she'd enter his place and be overwhelmed by sensations that had nothing to do with the present. In another time, with another man, with other men, this had happened before, so her senses would awaken to colors, smells, and sounds that were familiar. Soon she would be naked with him on a rough wool blanket thrown hastily over a cot. Her skin would be irritated by the wool, and she would discover his body and find it wonderful or not. He would devour her. He would say, I've never felt this way before. Or, you make me feel insane. She wouldn't like his work and would feel herself moving away from him. Already seen, it was in a way obscene, and ordinary. She calmly explained what shouldn't be seen, and why, and, as she did, found an old cave to enter.

Dr. Kaye didn't seem to appreciate her reluctance. Or if he did, in his subtle way he appeared to want her to have the experience, anyway. She knew she would go, then, to Rex's studio, and announced on the train that she'd be there Saturday night—date night, Rex said. He looked at her again, that way. But she knew it would hasten the end, like a death sentence for promise. Recently, Helen had awaited Timothy McVeigh's execution with terror, but it had come and gone. No one mentioned him anymore. Others were being killed—just a few injections, put them to sleep, stop their breathing, and it's done, they're gone. Things die so easily, she said. Then she listened to Dr. Kaye breathe.

Saturday night Helen rang the bell on Rex's Williamsburg studio. All around her, singles and couples wandered on a mission to have fun. Soon they'd go home, and the streets would be empty. Rex greeted her with a drink—a Mojito—which he knew she loved. His studio was bare, except for his work and books, even austere, and it was clean. The sweet, thick rum numbed her, and she prepared for the worst and the best. There was no in-between.

His paintings were, in a way, pictures of pictures. Unexpectedly, she responded to them, because they appreciated the distance between things. Then, without much talk, they had sex. She wasn't sure why, but resisting was harder. Rex adored her, her body, he was nimble and smelled like wet sand. He came, finally, but she didn't want to or couldn't. She held something back. Rex was bothered, and her head felt as if it had split apart. But it didn't matter in some way she couldn't explain to Dr. Kaye. She heard him move in his chair. She worried that he wasn't interested. Maybe her stories exhausted him. Rex called her every day. She wondered if she should find another man, one she couldn't have.

Chartreuse

How abrupt she was. She'd handed him the glass of Chartreuse, and her wrist flicked upward. Her hand's rebelling, he thought. Then she flinched. But she caught herself, she hadn't told him what actually happened, and she hadn't lied. She'd left room in their conversation for ambiguity. So this was the conversation he was in, but what about the others he hadn't been asked to join. His life was cycling into territory where gaps counted more. Mind the gap, but his mind was wandering.

"In La Grande-Chartreuse," she said, also abruptly but with a laugh, as if to distract him, "the head and celebrated monastery of the Carthusians, near Grenoble, the monks brewed Chartreuse. It's a liqueur or aperitif—you can have it before or after—made from aromatic herbs and brandy. The recipe is an ancient secret."

She visited the monastery years ago, crossing the Channel as a teenager, and pronounced the word "herb" the English way, its "h" heavy and funny as the man's name.

"Pope Victor III, Bruno of Cologne, founded the order in 1086. Twenty years after the Norman invasion..."

He interrupted her then, he remembered he interrupted her, and she hated that. "When the English language suffered a loss of prestige, but you still keep that hard 'h,' don't you?"

She drank some more, while he told her the color of Chartreuse looked sick, even feverish, but maybe the weird yellow and green high-voltage potion held an alluring illness, laced with the charge of deception. Her cheeks flared scarlet, the garish liqueur having its way with her. It burned his throat, too. But she kept her tongue, and her ruse, if it was one, wasn't even bruised. He wasn't going to force the issue, it would be like rape, and who wants truth or sex that way. He swallowed the yellow/green liqueur, distasteful and medicinal. Then he poured them both another Chartreuse.

A kind of golden amnesia stilled other monologues inside him. Her shirt, chartreuse for the occasion—their fifth anniversary—winked ambivalently. She liked designing their nights, he thought, color combinations were her thing. He wondered how he fit in some-times. Yellow elided with the green, never landing on the integrity of one color, and, he reflected sullenly, her blouse managed to be a fabric of lies, too. The silk looked sinister, too shiny, and, under the light, his wife's facade iridesced. Glimmering vile and then beautiful. Inconstant chartreuse numbed his tongue and his eyes.

"This tastes disgusting," he said, finally. "I could get used to it."

"Absinthe," she explained, or he remembered she did, "was called the green fairy, because it made everyone crazy—everyone became addicted, and there was legislation against it, still is, like against hero-in, because they thought it would destroy French civilization."

"Maybe it did."

"But now you can find it, if you want. At a party I went to we all drank from the fairy cup."

She didn't find his eyes. Maybe it was then, he thought, that it happened.

"The Carthusians were expelled from France in 1903, and they went to Tarragona. Spain."

"Home of tarragon?"

"But they returned in 1941." He remembered thinking about the Pope's treachery during the war.

Her blouse kept changing, now yellow, now green. It was kind of driving him crazy, but maybe it was the effect of Chartreuse. What she liked best about the Carthusian monks was their vow of absolute silence—it was the most rigorous order. Resolute religiosos, she joked, who, paradoxically, brewed a high-volume alcoholic drink. She figured they didn't indulge, because it might loosen their tongues.

"In 1960, there were only 537 Carthusians," she said.

"Your tongue isn't loose," he said.

"I'm thinking of going on a retreat—I want to be silent."

"Leave the conversation?" he asked.

"You're too ironic for words."

"You got me."

Just what he expected of her, to run; but what did he expect of her. He toasted her with the Manichean aperitif or liqueur, whatever it was. Her reticence settled over him like a green or yellow cloud. With it, she left. She spent half a year away, in silence, or at least she didn't talk to him. He had to trust her, he supposed. She stayed with a very small order of Carthusian nuns, who didn't drink Chartreuse. He condemned himself for not pursuing her there.

While she was away, he spoke of his perplexity to his therapist, who was not silent enough. Loyalty, betrayal, living with the lie, not escaping it, the way some fled from what was supposed to be true— he wrote notes to himself about honest disillusionment. To others, within this mostly quiet time, sometimes he was shameless and blatant. He once declared at a cocktail party, a fragile glass of Chartreuse—his drink now—in his hand, "Fidelity and infidelity, what's one without the other? You can't imagine a mountainless valley, can you?" With a secret-holder's thrill at disclosure, he told his therapist: "I love her. I live inside an illusion. A shimmering criminal illusion."

On weekends, he hit stores and developed the habit of collecting shirts and jackets of chartreuse. The dubious shade represented his obsession with transparency and opacity. Now he thought it was one thing, and he could see right through it and her. Then it was another, and she was denser than a black hole. He wished he were the Hubble telescope.

Chartreuse was popular, the new grey, he liked to say, and his closet was full when she returned. Her need for silence—at least with him—hadn't completely abated. He never knew if it was because she had once deceived him or because she couldn't stop. Or because his once having thought she did horrified her, when she hadn't, and now she wanted to and couldn't.

He contented himself with the little things, his and her chartreuse towels, how they equitably divided chores—the pleasure of domesticity stayed novel for him—and her occasional marital passion. Like him, she fashioned herself daily, a devotee of Harold Rosenberg's "tradition of the new." So eventually they would turn old-fashioned. At least, they were together.

He would always associate the night it happened, when he thought it happened, with fateful chartreuse, whose eternal shiftiness he could spin tales about. Also, about the CIA, the monastery as the first factory, and the beauty of silence. It was really golden. He and his wife celebrated themselves and their differences on their anniversary. They loved and denied each other, simultaneously, and more and more laughed at themselves. There were things he'd never know. Still, nothing competed with their complicity, their chartreuse hours together.

A Simple Idea

This happened a long time ago. My best friend was in Los Angeles, and she and I talked on the phone a lot. I urged her to move to New York, and finally she did. She drove cross-country, and when she arrived, she was told she didn't have to worry about the $10,000 in California parking tickets she had on her car. There was no reciprocity between the two states, she was told, so there was no way her car's outlaw status would be discovered in New York. The guy who told her said he was a cop. They met in a bar, then they had sex. Anyway, I think they did.

My friend started accumulating NYC tickets. Blithely, for a while. She shoved the tickets into the glove compartment. I suppose people kept gloves in those compartments at one time. When there was no room left, she threw them on the floor of her car. Then she decided she'd better find a parking lot. But she didn't want to pay hundreds of dollars for a space.

One day she noticed a parking lot near her house which was barred from entry by a heavy chain and lock. A week later she noticed a man walking to the lot. He used a key to unlock the gate. She got up her nerve and asked him if she could park there if she gave him some money. Would he make her a key? He said he'd think about it. The next day he telephoned her and said OK. So every month my friend handed the man $50 in a white business envelope. It was illegal, but she wasn't getting tickets from the City and throwing them on the floor of her car.

She was relatively happy parking in the lot, relieved anyway, because there was one less thing to worry about. But after a while she thought some of the other drivers—men going to work in the building attached to the lot—were looking at her weirdly, staring at her and her car. Some seemed menacing, she told me. But then she was paranoid. She knew that, so she decided not to act on her suspicions. Time passed. Time always passes.

One afternoon my friend received a call from a man who identified himself as a cop. He said, Hello, and used her first name, Sandra, and asked her sternly:

—Are you parking illegally, Sandra, because if you are, and you don't remove your car from the lot right now—I'm giving you ten minutes—I'll have to arrest you.

My friend hung up, threw on her coat, ran out the door to the lot, and drove her car far away. Then she phoned me and told me what happened. She was terrified. She thought the cop might show up and arrest her at any moment, she thought she'd be taken to jail.

—That was no cop, I said.

—How do you know? she asked.

—A cop wouldn't phone you and give you a warning, I answered. But I was worried that I might be wrong, and that she might be arrested.

—And he's not going to say he's going to give you a second chance, because you don't get second chances if you're doing something illegal and they find out, unless they're corrupt, and he wouldn't say, I'm a cop. He'd give his name and rank or something.

My friend listened, annoyed that I was calm, and she wasn't satisfied or convinced. She thought she might be under surveillance and would be busted later. She owed thousands of dollars in tickets in two states. It might be a sting operation, something convoluted. I had to convince her she was not in danger of going to jail. I told her I had an idea and hung up.

It was simple. I'd call a precinct and ask the desk cop how a cop would identify himself over the phone. I'd learn the protocol, how cops wouldn't do what that so-called cop had done, allay my friend's fears, and also show her I was taking her anxiety seriously.

I looked up precincts in the telephone book and chose one in the West Village, where I thought they'd be used to handling unusual questions.

—Tenth precinct, Sergeant Molloy, the desk cop said.

—Hi, I have a question, I said.

—Yeah.

—How do police identify themselves over the phone?

—What do you mean? Molloy asked.

—If a cop calls you, what does he say?

—What do you mean, what does he say?

—I mean, how does he say he's a policeman? What's the official way to do it? The desk cop was silent for a few seconds.

—A cop called you. What'd he say? What'd he want?

—He didn't call me, he called a friend.

—What did he say to your friend?

I couldn't hang up, because I wouldn't get the information I wanted. If I hung up, Molloy could have the call traced. I'd be in trouble for making harassing calls to precincts, which would be extremely ironic.

—He said to her… he said, Hello, I'm the police.

—Yeah. Then what?

—And then, then he said…

I didn't want to tell him the story, give my friend's real name, tell him about her tickets in two states, and her car being parked illegally, and her bribing the guy in the corporate lot. But I had to give him some sense of the situation in order to get the information I needed.

—He said to her, Hi, Diana. Hi, I'm the police. Then he said, he said, Diana… Diana… have you done anything wrong lately?

There was a very long silence.

—Have you done anything wrong lately? Molloy repeated.

It was weird coming from a cop's mouth. He gathered his thoughts, while I remained breathlessly quiet.

—A police officer wouldn't say that, Molloy answered soberly. A police officer wouldn't say that.

—He wouldn't, I repeated, just as gravely.

The cop thought again, for a longer time.

—Listen, I want you to let me know if he ever calls your friend again. Because a cop shouldn't do that… He trailed off.

—That guy's impersonating an officer.

—Oh, yeah. I'm sure he won't… he probably won't call her again. But if he does, I'll phone you immediately, I promise.

—You do that, Molloy said.

—I will. Thanks, I said.

—Yeah, he said. Maybe Molloy didn't believe any of this, but he did the whole thing straight.

I called my friend, and we stayed on the phone for hours, laughing about how crazy I was to say "Have you done anything wrong lately?" to a cop, with all its implications, and we laughed about her racing out of her house to the corporate lot, jumping into her car and driving off in search of a legal parking space as if she were being chased by the devil.

Maybe the devil was chasing her and me. Because we laughed off and on for about a year more, and then we had less to laugh about, and then nothing to laugh about. I don't know, we grew to distrust each other, and stopped being friends. Maybe Molloy laughed later.

Give Us Some Dirt

On long, summer nights in Pin Point, the Georgia air hung still as a corpse, and they'd wait for a breeze to save them. The heat felt like another skin on Clarence. His Mother would say, Clarence, what have you been up to? Playing by the river again? Oh Lord, we've got to clean you up for church, but aren't you something to behold? And his mother would clap her palms together or spread her arms wide, like their preacher. Oh, Lord, she'd exclaim. Sometimes she'd point to sister and lovingly scold, "She doesn't get up to trouble like you, son." Clarence scrubbed the mud off until his knuckles nearly bled, while his sister giggled.

These days she wasn't laughing so much.

The dirt couldn't be washed away, not after Clarence kneeled in their white church, and they slimed him with derision. They couldn't see who he was, how hard he'd worked, what he'd had to do, but he knew how to act. Behave yourself, boy, Daddy would say. Clarence's grandfather, Clarence called him Daddy, was a strict, righteous man, who never complained, not even during segregation times, didn't say a word, so Clarence wouldn't, either. Those days were over, and they had their freedom now. He set Daddy's bust on a shelf near his desk in his new office.

The D.C. nights mortified him, the air as suffocating as Pin

Point's. Clarence couldn't free himself of history's stench. On some interminable evenings, he nearly sent that woman a message, made the call, because she'd dragged him down for their delectation. He'd pick up the receiver and put it down.

The noise of the ceiling fan assaulted him like a swarm of bugs. Clarence's jaw locked, and his strong hands balled into fists. Every pornographic day of his trial, Clarence's wife, Virginia, sat quietly behind him. She barely moved for hours on end, didn't betray anything, and he worried that, if she had, the calumnies would have spread even further, and the sniggers and whispers would have ripped her and him to pieces. He rubbed his face, recalling her startling composure. Rigid, at attention, a soldier in his beleaguered army.

He didn't tell Virginia what the senators whispered—if he'd tried to marry her, if they'd had sex before the Court decided Loving v. Virginia, they'd have been arrested, and wasn't it ironic—the Court made Clarence's dick legal in Virginia, in Virginia? The Capitol's dirty joke. Their dry Yankee lips cracked into bloodless grins.

The room's high ceilings dwarfed him. Clarence glanced at a stack of legal papers. His wife was unassailable and white, but under their vicious spotlight her skin looked pasty and sick. She clung to him through his humiliation, even when disgrace lingered like the smell of shit. And now she bore the tainted mark with him.

Clarence had absorbed Daddy's lessons, he could keep everything inside, all of it. He watched his grandfather's bust, half expecting it to move, but it only stared down at him from the shelf. Clarence picked the receiver up again and put it down again. He was in that weird trance, and breathed in slowly, to calm himself, and breathed out slowly, to stay calm, and then closed his eyes. Clarence would leave that woman alone, leave her be, and, anyway, what was the sense, what was there to say years later, and there'd be consequences.

He was weary of scrubbing.

When he won, when the seat was his, he watched his friends' joy, black and white, and they embraced him, slapped him on the back—remember what's important, what it's for, our principles, it's all worth it. Clarence was the blackest Supreme Court justice in the land, the blackest this country would ever see. He held that inside him, too, and patted his round belly.

Clarence liked to joke about his heft, his gravitas, with his friends and the other Justices. When he delivered his rare speeches, he occasionally mentioned his girth, which drew a laugh, since his body was a source of mirth. Sometimes his hands rested on his stomach during sessions, when he was courtly if mute. The court watchers noted that he never asked questions, they remarked on it until they finally stopped. Clarence felt he didn't have to say a word. He'd talk if he wanted, and he preferred not to.

When his hair turned white, like Clinton's, that other fallen brother, Virginia said he looked distinguished, not old. Still, she worried about his weight, she didn't want to lose him. He hushed her. He intended to be on the bench as long as he could, at least as long as Thurgood Marshall. He looked at Daddy again, eternally silenced, and sometimes talked to him, telling him almost everything. Clarence could hear Daddy, he could hear his voice always. He knew what he'd say.

Clarence's trial bulged fat inside him. He'd never forget his ordeal, not a moment of it. He closed his briefcase and felt the urge to push Daddy from his perch. He would never let anyone forget his trial. Clarence chuckled suddenly, and a harsh, guttural noise escaped from him like a runaway slave. He'd have the last laugh, he was color blind, and they'd all pay in the end.

The title "Give Us Some Dirt" is taken from Clarence Thomas' testimony during the hearings, October 1991.

Playing Hurt

Abigail planned on retiring at forty and kidded around with her friends about how she'd better lay her golden eggs fast. But all bearers of wishes and jokes are also serious. In the future, she would be her own benevolent despot, spend what she had accumulated, and indulge herself. Maybe study Chinese or Arabic, certainly Latin, shave her head, if she wanted, because, literally, she would have earned it.

From her desk, Abigail reveled in the Chrysler Building's beautiful austerity, the sun dropping away in its own time. She admired nature's independence. Her Harvard Law School friends wondered why she worked in an investment bank, no adventure, no social meaning, they teased her, but she believed everyone had a right to happiness, and that took money. Mostly her friends came from privileged families and didn't have her special fervor, so, in a crucial way, they didn't get her. But as a scholarship student, Abigail grew up observing them and learned to recognize the secret operations of class and power.

Nathaniel Murphy walked past her glassed-in office. He still had most of his hair, his good looks, he was almost too handsome, though his nose had thickened since she'd first seen his picture when he was twenty-eight. The Internet golden boy had grown fleshier, even as his world had shrunk, but there he was in his Armani suit. She could smell his aftershave lotion, Vervain probably.

The numbers on the accounts blurred, Abigail pushed her glasses to the bridge of her nose, thrust her face closer to the papers, and self-consciously tugged on her short skirt. He was headed to the vault, distracted or worried, she thought, and he should be. He would soon open a security box, which probably held birth certificates, his parents' wills, some gold, jewelry, certificates. Abigail had helped the elder Mr. Murphy draw up his will; he had left most of his fortune to charitable foundations, but his son's fortune had vanished, along with other dot-commers.

Nathaniel Murphy stayed in her imagination. His fall had been dramatic, public, and she wondered at his profligacy and hubris. While the sun sank at its own speed, Abigail imagined the younger Murphy's hand hitting the sides of the metal security box. He was in a dark hole, yet everything surrounding him gleamed. He was like a character from a Patricia Highsmith novel, not Ripley, but others whose guilt registered on a human stock market. Abigail felt she had suffered too much to be guilty about anything, but Nathaniel had cost people millions, he'd wasted everything he had from birth and more. Being poor again terrified her, the thought made her sick, but he had no idea what it was like, and, rather than provoking resentment, it added allure to his mystery, even innocence.

The elder Mr. Murphy once revealed that Nate's wife had asked for a divorce right after the crash. He couldn't help him, Nate made terrible choices; he gambled, not invested; he's a playboy, his father confided, with time to kill. He's drinking too much, and the girls sail in and out of his life. She liked Mr. Murphy, who was a gentleman, but she would have protected his son better, guided him. Abigail kept close watch on her own money, talked to her broker daily, and flushed with warmth when, each month, she saw her accounts swell.

A guard closed the vault's massive doors behind Nate. He turned a corner and walked down a hall, where Abigail encountered him. Abigail hadn't planned it, she'd gone to the women's room, and their paths crossed. They had several times before, when they would nod indifferently, but Abigail was never indifferent, she'd admit later. This time she stopped, and he did also.

—I'm sorry about your father, I liked him, Abigail said.

—Thank you, he said. He liked you, too.

She had never noticed how green his brown eyes were, almost olive, then she realized they were just standing, not talking, and she must have been staring into his eyes. She tugged at her short skirt, meaning to return to her office, when he smiled familiarly at her.

—You like it here?

—Sure, I'm here, yes, I do.

—They let you wear short skirts.

—I wear what I want.

Five weeks later, the younger Mr. Murphy moved in.

That first night in a corner of the bar at the Hotel Pierre, Nathaniel kissed her with restrained ardor, and Abigail knew much more inhabited him. He told her about his insecurity because of his father's reputation, she told him her mother cleaned houses, her father couldn't keep a job. But what mattered was being close to him. The next night, he whispered words that infuriated her, yet her breath stopped anyway. He'd been in love with her since he first saw her, his father told him she was the one, and with him her life would be happy—I am happy, she said—he could make her happier, babies, if she wanted, millions of orgasms. I've heard that in hundreds of movies, Abigail said, maybe not the bit about orgasms. After he kissed her without restraint, Abigail lost the sense of where she was. I'm not a movie, Nathaniel muttered into her ear, I'm just a soft touch for you. Curiously, she saw old Mr. Murphy in him.

You're the soft touch, her friends insisted, you're nuts, he'll screw you. They'd never seen Abigail like this, she had never felt like this. You'll wash his stocks at night, her best friend quipped, but nothing swayed Abigail. Against her exasperated friends' advice, Nate moved in.

They were happy. What her friends hadn't realized was that Nate was crazy about Abigail, devoted. He lived up to his promises, she told them, he quit drinking completely, and every week he took meetings with smart entrepreneurs like himself. She knew both his desire and his drive, they both loved the game of business, and she adored him, he made her swoon. With her, she knew he'd succeed, and Nate told her he'd thrown away his little black book. But Nate had seen that in too many corny movies, so actually it went into the security box, a document of his bachelorhood, Abigail wouldn't mind.

They married in a mauve room in the Hotel Pierre, where her friends and his celebrated, his dotty mother in attendance, Abigail's family discreetly absent. A few days before, almost as a joke, they had signed a prenuptial agreement. It didn't mean anything; she was a lawyer, that was all. The newlyweds were delirious. She felt sexy and content with him, he felt like a man again.

Abigail's clients loved her, she helped them, a few lost big, there was some ruin, some bankruptcies, but, bottom line, she made money for the firm. A partnership came next. There was hardly time for sex, though Nate persisted in wanting to add to Abigail's orgasm account, as they called it. She turned him away once, saying, I'd prefer you made money, like, Make money not love. He was shocked and angry, and she took it back, but he was hurt, even wounded. You're soft, his father used to say, toughen up. Abigail tried to soothe him, but really she wanted him working, back on his feet, emotional support was one thing, financial another. She saw him retreat a little, but he'd come back, he'd understand. She didn't notice his drinking, he hid it, doing it only when she was at work or asleep. Now, less and less, he wanted to have sex, and she was too tired anyway.

Nate's best friend at Princeton called with a brilliant idea, and since Nate owned the sharpest biz head he knew, he wanted him as a partner, if Nate liked what he heard, and he did—an environmentally important and scientifically significant venture to develop microbes that absorb waste in the ocean. Nate needed a couple of million to invest, not much really, but he didn't have it. He would borrow it from Abigail, be told his friend, he'd pay her back when the business saw its first profits. She trusts me, Nate told him.

Later, Abigail unlocked the door to Nate's embrace. He repeated the conversation, every word, with embellishment more bubbly than the champagne he'd opened. She looked into his olive eyes, at his too-handsome face, and her friends' and his father's admonitions returned, as if written upon that face. He would use her, leave her, he'd take her money, he was a playboy. She fought her fear, an instinct maybe, after all she must love Nate, her husband, she should help him to succeed. Even so, she told him she needed time to think, because that kind of money was serious. Nate was stunned. Abigail saw disbelief in his eyes or weakness, like in her father's eyes, a beaten dog's eyes, in bed, far from Nate, Abigail dreamed someone was trying to kill her. Nate couldn't sleep.

Some days later, Nate said there's gold in the security box, grandmother's jewelry, take it as collateral. She hated his pleading, his putting her in an impossible position, he knew she had to protect her future. What if, she thought, what if... and she wasn't being selfish, life was unpredictable. She wondered why she'd ever fallen in love with him, he didn't know her at all. A hardness insinuated itself inside her, and a space opened between them that was palpable to Nate. He appeared to wither before her eyes, too insecure, she realized, he's nothing like his father. She couldn't name what he was doing to her, but it was wrong, everything about him and her felt wrong. Meanwhile, Nate's potential partner waited, an intrepid humiliation returned, and Nate even drank in front of Abigail.

Still, Abigail suppressed her nameless protests and went with him to open the security box. It was strange walking down the hall where they'd first talked and fallen in love, but more terrible she felt it was her death march. The guard opened the door, and Nate and she entered the vault, where two straight-backed chairs were brought to them and then the gray steel box. There was some jewelry, she could have it appraised, some certificates, gold, and bonds. Nate lifted one up to show her, and beneath it lay his little black book. When Abigail reached for it, Nate put his hand on her arm.

—It doesn't mean anything, I kept it like a scrapbook.

She shook his hand off.

—You lied to me.

She rose, his address book in her hand, evidence of everything she'd been thinking, no one could blame her, she wasn't responsible, leaving him wasn't selfish. But it meant nothing, he repeated the next day. It means everything, she repeated, she could never trust him again. He claimed she already didn't, she wouldn't lend him money, she insisted that he wouldn't have asked for it if he really loved her. She wanted a divorce.

—You never loved me, he said.

—That isn't true, I can't ever trust you again.

To Nate, her abandonment confirmed his father's bad opinion of him, and also that his past had caught up to him, it always would. Abigail had to protect herself, no matter what, he didn't understand. Their prenuptial agreement made divorce relatively easy, and she was so calm, her friends believed she was in shock, but his betrayal had been awful, they all agreed. When Abigail heard he'd returned to all his old ways, proving her right, that he would've just dragged her down, she felt sad but also secure in herself. And she was herself again, her friends thought, especially because Abigail volunteered at an animal shelter on weekends and fed strays on the street as she had during law school. When people at the office asked why, she'd explain she trusted cats and dogs, humans domesticated them, so they're defenseless without us. But people, she occasionally added, people usually deserve what they get.

More Sex

There were many men she wanted to have sex with, some days more men than other days, though she'd already had sex with many men, but those were the ones who were easy to have sex with or to find for sex, since they lived in the neighborhood; she could meet them at parties or in clubs, even in grocery stores, especially near the beer, wine, and cheese displays, probably because they're often served at parties. It was easy to find men for sex, because she knew that men think about sex all the time, or every seven minutes, so they're always ready for sex. She had read the seven-minute statistic in the *Times* science section some years back and wondered about it. Then she experimented with herself. She set a timer for seven minutes throughout five hours, when she was home, and, whatever she was doing, reading, eating, washing dishes, looking at the ceiling or out of the window, when the alarm went off, she thought about sex. Every seven minutes, she realized, was very frequent, and, if she were feeling sad, it was hard to think about sex, and also she realized she didn't think about sex, maybe she didn't know how, and she managed poorly or inadequately to concoct an image or something or someone to fantasize about. Every seven minutes was hard, she didn't know how men did it, because she didn't have that kind of imagination, and also she didn't know for how long men thought about sex every seven minutes. And what did they think up? Their penis entering a woman's vagina, if they were heterosexual, while she's moaning, Fuck me, fuck me hard, and was it always the same? Her lack of sexual imagination was one of the reasons she liked going to the movies. There was usually sex in the movies she saw, sometimes lots of it, if it was unrated or X-rated, and sometimes there was soft-core porn-like sex in movies, in so-called love scenes, which activated her dormant, lackluster, or empty fantasy life, but then she often became infatuated with the lead actor and, for a while, she pictured having sex with him. Many of the men she wanted to have sex with were actors, especially those who were good lovers in movies and sometimes on TV. They appeared to be good at sex, although that was hard to define, she didn't know if it was similar to being good at tennis or some other activity; anyway, to her, inexactly, it was the way they held a female actor, the way they looked into her eyes, the kind of passion they exuded, and, manufactured or not, the sex or passion seemed real to her. She hoped they were really good at sex and not just acting, although actual people do act when having sex, too, though why they do and for what purpose, she wasn't sure. It wasn't only faking orgasms, which women were said to do to make men feel better or just to get them to stop, since they really weren't having any pleasure anyway. Men acted during sex, too, she knew several, some were worse actors than others. But the men she wanted to have sex with, the actual actors, were not available to her, they were in Hollywood, or London, or they were sometimes on the streets of New York City, like Sean Connery, but he was old when she saw him, and Michael Imperioli from *The Sopranos*, but she had never wanted to have sex with him, he was weaselly, even if she felt sorry for him in his part, and Al Pacino, she'd seen him in an Italian restaurant where he walked around in dark glasses as if he

.

didn't want anyone looking at him but made such a show of it everyone recognized him, though no one said hello or anything to him, because few do that in New York, mostly people don't. But none of these actors she had seen in person appealed to her. She wanted to have sex with Daniel Day-Lewis, but only as he was when he played an American Indian/Caucasian in *The Last of the Mohicans*, not in any of his other roles, he was never again a barechested, mostly silent Indian, and now he didn't want to act, she heard, and was a shoemaker, and then for a while she wanted sex with David Caruso, when he was on TV in *NYPD Blue*, because he could do tenderness and seemed gentle and also lusty, but then he quit the show, and she heard he was the opposite of that role, an egomaniacal asshole, and she did not want to have sex with George Clooney, Sean Penn, Tom Hanks, Ralph Fiennes, countless others, even McDreamy in *Grey's Anatomy*, because everyone wanted him, and that made him much too common, and in her fantasies, when she could cook one up, she would have had to compete with too many women—and men, probably—for him. There were so many she didn't want to have sex with that sometimes going to the movies was as disappointing as real sex with actual non-actor—though, on occasion—acting men. But wanting to have sex with men she couldn't have, because they weren't around ever, and would ignore her in favor of another actor, male or female, was also all right, because she could easily have sex with men she didn't necessarily want, and they weren't so bad, really. She could ask them about what pictures they had in their minds every seven minutes, and she didn't think she could do that with movie stars.

Dear Ollie

Dear Ollie,

It's been a long time. I think of you sometimes, and I know you think of me. I take a perverse satisfaction in that, even in the jaded ways you disguise me in your so-called fictions. I really don't care. But I just read your "manifesto against the past." No one "votes for guilt." I also have "funny mental pictures" of that mansion we lived in on the Hudson. It wasn't "haunted," except by an unghostly Timothy Leary. Everyone said he dropped acid there. Everyone said they used to have wild parties. Even back then the term wild parties bothered me. No one ever gave details.

You and I were the only non-psych students living in the mansion. You and they were older, graduate students, but they were all research psychologists and thought everyone else was crazy, so they devised experiments to prove it. There was that one sullen guy who worked with rats. He had a big room near mine. I used to look in as I passed it. He kept his shoes under the chair of his desk in a certain way, everything in his room had a specific order, and if his shoes were moved even a quarter inch, he went crazy.

Remember when he drove his car into a wall? Then he disappeared. Remember it's my past, too, you want to "throw into the garbage, to be carted away by muscular men and sent floating on a barge to North Carolina.

One night, you brought a friend home from Juilliard, a fellow student. If you recall, our dining room had dark walls and no electricity. We ate by candlelight—there were many candles in different states of meltdown on the long table that night. About ten, I think.

Before dinner, one of the research psychologists suggested it'd be fun to put blue vegetable dye in the mashed potatoes. Your friend wouldn't know. We'd act as if the potatoes weren't blue, just the usual white, and even though your friend might protest and insist they were blue, we'd keeping insisting they were white. We'd just pretend he was crazy for thinking they were blue. We cooked this up in the kitchen. When you came in with him, someone took you aside and told you. You went along with it. Everyone has a streak of sadism, one of the psych guys said.

I don't remember who brought in the potatoes, we all participated, though, and then we all sat down around the big wooden table. The blue mashed potatoes were served in a glass bowl. Even by candlelight, they were bright blue.

We passed the food. When the bowl of blue potatoes reached your friend, he reacted with delight. Blue mashed potatoes, he said. Someone said, They're not blue. Your friend said, They're not? They look blue. Someone else said, No, they're not. You were sitting next to him.

The potatoes kept going around. Your friend said, again, They really look blue. Everyone acted as if nothing was happening. Your friend kept looking at the bowl. He became visibly agitated. He said, They look blue. Someone said, Maybe it's the candlelight. The flames have a bluish tinge. Your friend kept looking, squinting his eyes. Then he insisted, They look blue to me. Someone said, with annoyance, Would you stop it? They're not blue. Your friend turned quiet. He kept looking, though, and we all kept eating.

The coup de grâce, I guess you'd call it, was dessert. In the kitchen, someone decided to dye the milk blue. The cake, coffee, and blue milk were brought to the table. We served the blue milk in a glass pitcher. No one said much as the pitcher went around the table. Your friend watched silently. When it came to him, he stared at the pitcher and poured the blue milk into his coffee. This time, he said nothing. Nothing. At that point I ran into the kitchen. I couldn't control myself.

Later, you told him. After dinner, when you were alone with him, you told him. But I'm wondering, after all these years, did he ever forgive you? What happened to him? Does he still play the trombone?

You were good, Ollie. But somehow, in "regurgitating the past and moving on," I'm "the reckless prankster" whose "promiscuous heart" you broke. The only thing in that house you ever broke was your musician friend and crazy Roger's green plates.

Whatever,
Lynne Tillman
NEW YORK, NEW YORK

But There's a Family Resemblance

There's a story in my family about Great Uncle Charley, who didn't know, until he was eighteen and married Margaret, that women went to the bathroom. It's always told with that euphemism. My father, whose uncle Charley was, told it to me when I was thirteen, in a father-son rite of passage, his three brothers told their sons and, later, even their daughters, when they loosened up about girls.

When Charley and his brothers were kids, they made up their own basketball team in the Not-So-Tall League, they were all under 5' 8". They even had shirts made up; there are six photos of that. I'm named after Great Uncle Charley, they say he guarded like a wild dog. My dad's generation is taller, mine even taller, except for my twin sisters. They're short, in every snapshot they look like dwarfs. I pored over the family albums starting when I was a kid; I think it was because I was the youngest and needed to get up to speed fast. I knocked into furniture all the time, too, because I raced around, not looking where I was going, running from everything as if a monster would get me. I'm still covered in bruises.

When I think about Great Uncle Charley's shock at seeing his blushing bride, Margaret, on the can for the first time, I can visualize it, like a snapshot, but I never knew him, he died before I was born. They say you can't know the other, you can't know yourself, and sometimes you don't want to know the other or yourself. I'm sick of trying and failing. But when I imagine my namesake, I can see a smile and a robust body, because of the family pictures, and I always ask myself: could Uncle Charlie have had any kind of a sex life after that? I don't know why they named me after him, I'm not like him, according to my mother, but I feel implicated in his sexual ignorance. Families do that, implicate you in them. There are the twins, and one boy ahead of me, he's the oldest, and we're separated, oldest to youngest, by six years, so my mother was kept busy, but my father was the boss at home and in the world. He owned a paper factory, and I developed a love for paper, because he'd bring home samples; I liked to touch them, especially the glossy kind, photographic paper, which I licked until one day my mother shouted, "Stop that. You'll get cancer." So I stopped.

After Charley died, a terrible secret exploded on Aunt Margaret, who had a near-fatal heart attack and became an invalid, and then she died when I was ten. My parents still won't tell me what happened. Neither will Stella, Charley and Margaret's only daughter, tall and willowy, and strangely silent about everything. Maybe she doesn't know.

I have a doctorate in cultural anthropology and am a tenured associate professor—the big baby can't be fired, my brother likes to joke—and teach my students that a family's implicit contract is to keep its secrets. They're essential to the kinship bond, which offers protection at a price—loyalty to blood and brood. What happens in the family stays there: no obedience, no protection. I use various media to explain certain phenomena and enduring characteristics, as well as new adaptations, of the American family. For example, Mafia movies succeeded, after the family was hammered during the 1960s, by promoting oaths that, like marriage, were 'til death do you part, while guilt and criminality occurred only by disregarding the Family, not the law. The movies glorified the thugs' loyalty to the clan, but HBO's *The Sopranos* portrayed mob boss Tony Soprano's sadism so graphically that, Sunday by Sunday, the viewer's sympathy was shredded. But other genres will fill the bill, there'll be no end to war stories for an age of permanent war, and, with the cry for blind patriotism, an American's fidelity to family can be converted into an uncritical devotion to country.

My whole life, I've been absorbed in the family photo albums, home movies, and videos, classifying and preserving them, yet each time I look at my mother when she was nine, I stare, rapt: what's that expression, I wonder. Time passes in looking, I don't know how long, and the same fantasy occurs: I might see her static face move, speak, explain herself to me; in the videos, when my father sits at the head of the table at holidays, I see his contempt and malevolence and despise him even more. The few photographs I myself shot of him he hated, he said I made him look bad, that he didn't look like that, and tore them up in front of me. It's more evidence of his aggression to me.

At home, I study the familiar images, but in the end nothing changes, the movies run along the way they always do, and without close-ups, it's hard to see their faces, too many people are walking away from the camera, and the photographs don't open up, either, their surfaces are like closed doors, as mysterious as they were when I first saw them. I'm not sure what I'm looking for, that's the most honest response to explain my mania. I look and wait. The unguarded moments are the best, they're most available to interpretation and also to no interpretation, but always they remain unguarded moments that I can make more of, just the way I want to make more of my life. Instead, I'm facing their ambiguity, which may be truer. I also collect snapshots and albums of unknown people. My pleasure is that I don't know them, their anonymity identifies them to me, and, in a sense, through them, I can recognize my anonymity to others. It's like making yourself a stranger.

The American family sustains itself and mutates along with its movies, TV sitcoms, photographs, video. Since the 1960s, in tandem with political agitation, media have remade it, blood ties are no longer necessary, but family cohesion still requires loyalty and secrecy. Any gay/straight sitcom pledges allegiance to the same flag. And though the worst things happen in families, the most disgusting and painful, with long legacies, the family is still idealized; there's no replacement yet. It remains necessary for survival, and if you're not in one, your fate is usually worse. Children in London, taken away from their parents in the Blitz, sent to the countryside for safety, were more traumatized than those who stayed home during the bombings. No matter what kind of terrorism happens in a family, relatives hardly ever betray their families' secrets. The exceptions become sensations— Roseanne, La Toya Jackson. A member's self-interest can break any contract, implicit or explicit, in the name of honesty, to cure the family or to get just desserts.

Uncle Jack tried to sell life insurance after Uncle Jerry's funeral, and then my father stopped speaking to him. It's nothing to the big world, but the break reverberated in ours, loud, disturbing, and still does. What about weddings? How does the tribe meet, on whose territory? When my oldest first cousin, Betsy, married a black man, only the adults knew. We kids were told Betsy had done something wrong and went away. I figured she'd had an illegitimate baby, as it was called then, but after three beautiful legitimate kids with him, a nice guy, nicer than Betsy, her bigoted father relented, so she was back in the fold, times had changed—look who came to dinner in the movies and lived in big houses on TV. Her kids have refused to have anything to do with us. I don't blame them.

In the 1970s, the Loud family fascinated Americans with its psychological honesty, so compared with it, today's reality TV is a joke; it trivializes whatever reality you're invested in. The Louds fell apart afterward. TV's exhibitionists challenge credulity, sanity, yet people humiliate and shame themselves daily. Americans can't shake their Puritan past, so everyone's hoping to confess their sins and find God's grace. Still, it's hard to understand Judge Judy's appeal to the characters who want to be judged on TV, and those who watch manifest people's perverse, insatiable curiosity and schadenfreude. Also, some people miss being yelled at as they were in their families. I'm one of them.

Shame is different from thirty years ago, it doesn't last as long—Pee-Wee Herman, Martha Stewart, Richard Nixon—they bounced back, and, like history, Americans forget their pasts and sins quickly. Americans have several acts, with shame's mutation, and if they're televisual, it helps; if they're not, some can escape the stigma of being "ugly as sin" with plastic surgery—see Paula Jones and Linda Tripp. "Ugly" is bad, it's evil—remember what the bad guys in movies look like.

Great Uncle Charley lived with a secret, and there are more in my family: my brother discovered he'd been born an androgyne, changed to a boy surgically, a fact hidden from him by my parents, until he began to date and felt weird emotions; the twins had abortions when they were fourteen, and apart from that "sin," they had sex with the same man, maybe at the same time; and my father hit my mother. Mom was frightened of him when he drank, she cowered, I remember her crouched, it's an image gelled in memory. We kids didn't need to be told, Keep your damn mouth shut, we knew. If I ratted, a term I learned from cop shows, I knew I was betraying Us, and I'd go to hell. So you're implicated in your family, always.

Mostly, my mother took the pictures. My father thought it was beneath him, he felt superior to us. My brother and I stood next to each other in many photos; he loomed over me until I turned fourteen and shot up ten inches. I became taller. He hated that, you can see it, I can, because I know his expressions. You can see, I can, the power balance shift: in later photos, then no photos, except at weddings, when we stood far apart, especially at his wedding. To my father's disgust, he married Claudia, born Claude, a male-to-female trannie; only close friends and family knew. My sisters loved being photographed together, they still do. The twins are identical, both pretty, one has fuller lips, the other a wider nose; you can tell them apart easily if you know them. Their entire lives they've looked at each other, images of each other, maybe wondering who's prettier, and whether she loves herself and image more or less than the other twin does.

The concept of family resemblance is reasonable, given genetics, but it's peculiar, because what makes a resemblance isn't clear, there's no feature-by-feature similarity. Most of us in families share a resemblance. Fascination with the "family other"—a neologism I used in my first book, *You're a Picture, You're Not a Picture*—is dulled by the other's being related by blood; yet what's near can be farther (what's in the mirror is farther than you think), because up close, we're less able to see each other. I don't look like my brother, but everyone says I do. I hate my brother, often we hate our siblings, so a family resemblance colludes against your difference against your will. Blood tells the story, it seems to say, of which you are a part, and like tragedy can't be escaped.

But what does comedy tell? Like about Great Uncle Charley, the buffoon, comic, teaser, the man who didn't know that women piss and shit. Or was his life a tragedy? Was there an inevitability to it? In comedy, the only inevitability is surprise, an unforeseen punch line; guess it, and it's not funny. Uncle Charley—his life's a toss up, he was always funny, everyone said, then he died and his terrible secret came out that wasn't funny, and it was a surprise. Tragedy can't be a complete shock; it must build and build to a foreseeable end, which can't ever be avoided. I can't see any of it in the family photographs. But a family resemblance shares that attribute—it can't be avoided. You can't escape what it says about you.

After people die, my mother put it, all that remains are photographs, that's why we take them. Then she said to me, more sharply, Your interest in the family photos is morbid, the photos, videos, you're holding on to your childhood, it's sick. I ignored her and still do, even though she's dead. Often when people die, you reconsider their statements. I just look at their pictures.

Time goes on, your sacred films and tapes of weddings and communions are hidden away, everyone wants to have them, few look at them again, most are just kept images. I hardly knew so-and-so, there she is forever, but I don't have to look at her, either. The matte or glossy snapshots, in a drawer or album, represent a past, stand as an implacable memory, stored away against time, and even if in time you recognize no one and nothing by them, even if you have the memory only because the photo exists, it's a kind of elegy to a reality, a fact or document from the distant past, a memento mori. Or, as Claire's ghost-brother Nate whispered to her in the finale of HBO's *Six Feet Under*, when she was shooting their family before leaving home, "That's already gone."

When they die, even clowns sometimes morph into tragic heroes. Take Great Uncle Charley. I stare at his photos, ranging from when he was three, posing for a professional in town, sticking his finger up his nose in a high school graduation photograph, his eyes bugging out at a party after his college graduation, looking boisterous with the Not-So-Tall basketball team, or beaming as he cuts the cake with his bride, Margaret, and on and on. Three years before he died, there's an arresting one of him with his head drooping to the side, a melancholy expression on his face. I want to peel away the emulsion, get under that sad-sack image, and find out his secret. It's a primitive urge maybe, or a silly or naive feeling, but no matter what I might seem to know about the fiction and illusion of images, I'm also still that little boy rushing around, curious, trying to find out what's what, and who, like Great Uncle Charley, is shocked at what I see that no one told me would be there. I want other pictures to efface what I do know, to show me another world, I want to kill images, burn them, like some of my brother. Photographs aren't real that way.

In my next book, I'm broaching treacherous ground and taking up some cultural questions around images, specifically, a photographer's disposition—the subject behind the camera—and the effects of family resemblance. When an artist pictures a family member, what's the psychological impact of a family resemblance on the artist? Is the image also a self-portrait, when the shooter "resembles" the one who poses and so also sees himself or herself? How does the sociology of the American family—for instance, sibling order—affect images? Whose "I"/"eye" can be trusted, if trust is an issue in art, and why? From what I learned in my family, I don't trust anyone in front of or behind a camera, but with a nod to its futility, I'll try to keep my bias out of it.

The Original Impulse

He appeared in her sleep like a regular. Sometimes she saw the actual
him on the street, then he appeared two, three nights in a row; on
the street, because he remembered her vaguely or well enough, it was
awkward.

Years ago they'd done a fast dance. Back then, when she studied
photography, she believed artists were constitutionally honest; but
his thrill had its own finish line. She missed classes, stayed out too
late, ate too much, and dormant neuroses fired. She expected a man
to love her the way her father did, explosively, devotedly. Months
later, near where they'd first met, she ignored him; he rushed after
her and apologized. Maybe he knew how bad it felt, but she never
said anything. He phoned sometimes, they drove around, drank coffee, talked, not about lies, and two years passed like that, haplessly,
when something obscene must have gone down, because he didn't
call again. What words were there for nothing. Nothing.

Her time was full, adequate, hollow, fine, and she felt content
enough with love and work, but no one lives in the present except
amnesiacs. Her history was a bracelet of holes around her wrist, not
a charm bracelet like her mother had worn; that was gone. Someone
had stolen it as her mother slipped away. It might be on that woman's
wrist now, the gold rectangular calendar hanging from it, a ruby stud-
ding her mother's birthdate, a reminder she wouldn't want. It would

weigh even more with blanks filled in by anonymous dead people.

Insignificant coincidences—the actual him in a hotel lobby, a bookstore doorway, crossing a street—made loose days feel planned. She moved forward, a smart phone to her ear or its small screen to her face, and anything might happen. She read a story he'd written about an accidental meeting with a woman from his protagonist's past. First he didn't recognize her, she'd changed so much from how he remembered her; then he felt something again, maybe for the woman, mostly for himself.

When he spotted her, she wondered if he felt sick alarm too. One Saturday, she didn't notice he was walking by, watching her, and when she looked up, aware of something, she half-smiled involuntarily. That could have meant anything, there was no true recognition from either of them. Without it, she couldn't perform retrospective miracles, transform traitors into saviors. When ex-friends' faces arose, stirred by the perfume of past time, they looked as they did back then. One of them, she heard, did look the same, because she'd already been lifted. But some things can't be lifted.

Abysses and miseries called down their own last judgments upon themselves. Katherine could recite many of her bad acts; it would be easy to locate her putative wounded and apologize like someone in AA, but what substance had she abused. Love, probably. Most likely they'd claim they had moved on and forgotten her. Besides, they might say, you never really meant that much to me. Or, let's be friends on Facebook. When the 20th-year reunion committee of her high school found her, she didn't respond. Formal invitations, phone messages. They insisted her absence would destroy the entire reason for the event. The date approached. She wondered if showing up might help adjudicate the past, and curiosity arched its back. She caught a ride with a popular girl who'd gone steady with a future movie star who'd had a pathetic end. The woman wore the same makeup she'd worn then, her eyes lined slyly with black. Startling, what gets kept.

The reunion was held in the town's best country club, and in front of the table with name badges, she sank, just the way she had growing up. Someone called to her, "Kat, Kat," and another, "Kat," while another fondly blasted "Kat" into her ear, someone whose name she didn't recognize even looking at the name badge. Indignant, the girl/woman pronounced her unmarried name as if the tribe were extinct. "And I'm called Katherine now," she answered. Throughout the night, they called her Kat as if she were still one of them.

Faces had been modified, some looked aged; all the boys looked older than the girls. Provincial, well-off, neither sex could believe she wasn't married, and she encouraged their bewilderment, eventually admitting she lived with someone. But no, no, she wasn't married. The girls especially looked at her pityingly, the boys lasciviously. One had been her sixth-grade boyfriend; he'd been pudgy but now his girth wasn't boyish or expectant. During cocktails, she huddled with the black kids, the minority in town, and sat at their dinner table, still a minority. Days later, some of her former friends telephoned. One announced gravely, "I told my daughter to be like you, not me." She didn't ask why. Her pudgy sixth-grade boyfriend decided he'd ruined her life, that's why she hadn't married. He thought because she hadn't married, she must be a tormented lesbian. Katherine remembered breaking up with him for a seventh-grader.

On an accidental corner, the night-time man's spectral presence tugged at her, a leash pulling in the wrong direction. If she existed as a translation from an unforgiving past, he must, too, but translation was too dainty for what had happened to her, or him, she supposed. Words weren't patches, and the nights didn't let up, repetition after repetition, but how many ways could he appear, in how many iterations: his cheek pressed against hers, his glance, like a pardon from their past, his sexy compassion—they both had been alive then.

She heard he treated his wife badly, but they might have an open marriage, blind oxymoron. She supposed he lied to his wife, a famous rock singer past her prime, the way he was. On an impulse, he might abandon the singer, no longer the blooming girl who'd obliterated his mortality. The singer might want to divorce him but won't, because of their child, or because she doesn't care about his infidelities, since she's had her own, or none, or because she can't bear another split when suturing wouldn't hold after so much scar tissue. What had their life meant, and, anyway, he always returned remorseful or defiant, or both.

Sometimes, passing a building or café, Katherine would recollect a doorway encounter like the one on Fifth Avenue where Lily Bart was spotted by Lawrence Selden and doomed. Behind that red door, in that bodega, in that high-rise on the eightieth floor, strangers and intimates lavished attention or withdrew it, or she did. She had entertained various kinds of intercourse, and the words spoken lay redacted under thick, black lines. She retrieved bits through the interstices of nodding heads.

A delicate young man trembled at the edge of recognition, but his face was now speckled like an old photograph.

She was eighteen and lay in the arms of a married man who respected, he said, her innocence, and held her close, saying he'd always remember this moment, but she wouldn't, because she didn't know how beautiful she was. There was a cool slip of a rough tongue on an inner thigh and a sensational confession. There was a Southerner whose sexuality was fiercely, erotically ambiguous. He stayed in her bed too long. She roared here and soared there, dwarfed by three massive white columns as she and her best college friend mugged before a filmless camera.

People often move away from cities and towns when reminiscences create profound debt and mortgage the future. They visit occasionally and discover that the debt has multiplied. Katherine stayed where she was, in her city, along with a majority of others who resolutely called it home and became teachers, therapists, florists, criminals, food professionals, homeless, or worked with immigrants and refugees, the way she did.

Her photographs had been in two one-person shows and several group exhibitions, but Katherine stopped taking her work seriously because, primarily, she couldn't convince herself that her images were better than anyone else's. The decisive moment was an indecisive one for her. She earned a degree in social work and dallied with becoming a psychoanalyst, but decided she didn't want to work with people too much like herself. The agency where she spent five days a week, with occasional nights of overtime because of the exigencies of desperate people's lives, suited her. The agency was respected and privately funded by well-known philanthropists. Every day people entered the office with foreign-born stories of violence, terror, and humiliation; her shame was nothing compared with theirs.

Two months after the high school reunion, one of the girls telephoned to remind Katherine, agonistically, of why their friendship had ended—remember, the friend urged, senior year. The friend cited her mother's dying of cancer, her boyfriend's betrayals--she married him anyway—but all this pain had forced her to abandon their friendship. "I couldn't help you," she said, "we couldn't help each other." The friend talked and talked until her voice fell off a cliff. So that was that.

Katherine never thought about that friend or her dying mother, but now she pretended to stroll from her childhood house on Butler up Adelaide Avenue to the street—Randolph—and the door of her friend's home. The lawn was wide and green, so it must have been spring, when sad things occur ironically. She didn't open the front door, she didn't want to walk up the carpeted staircase and see her friend cradling her dying mother. The front door swung open, anyway. Her friend's father had his back to her, at the dining room table, his old head supported in her young friend's hands. Now the friend turned toward her, disrupting the image, and Katherine ran home. Did that happen?

There he was again. Katherine was sitting on a couch in a lobby, waiting for a friend. She heard his voice, he strode to the elevator, and she didn't move, her face averted. He looked her way; she didn't relax her pose. It didn't matter if the night-time man knew her as she was now. He was a thorn pricking her side, that's all. Another of his stories appeared, and she read about the protagonist's having once received a postcard from a girl he'd been cheating with; his wife found it, and it ruined things between them for a while. He never saw the girl again. How true was he being, or could he be. He was faithless, but probably he didn't think so, not in the obvious ways. He bore an unfathomable loneliness, and he was faithful, in his way, to that.

At the agency, she listened to stories more terrible than the Greek tragedies she loved. When she learned that some friends didn't return to the books they'd cherished in school, she understood that some people lived as if the past were over. Been there, done that—she didn't know how. The Greeks would have his wife lose her voice, never to sing or even speak again. He'd suffer a downfall, realizing his hubris necessarily too late, and kill himself. The wife might kill herself too, but not harm their beautiful daughter, who would turn vengeful, without knowing whom to blame, unalterable fate swallowing her whole.

The night-time man played his role in her romance, reciting his few lines. She told no one, because dreams signify nothing to anyone else, and their accidental meetings were psychic jokes—those sidewalk and doorway scenes, the questions they raised, when she compared her life with his, what had occurred between then and now, all to test her self-made being. Startling, what gets kept.

On a dull February morning, a man entered the agency. Curiously, he recognized her name, because ten years back he'd seen her photographs in London, when he was covering culture for an Indian newspaper. He had a work visa—he was a journalist and visiting academic—but he wanted to bring his extended family from Bangladesh. He needed permanent residency, there were political issues, he knew important people and could get letters. He was charming, somewhat coy, especially when announcing that he suffered the curse of a minority writer. She asked what that was. She never presumed anything in the office.

"To be expected to write like a minority," he said.

"How do you mean."

"You must write of suffering with some nobility—you people expect authenticity. I bet you first heard about Bangladesh when George Harrison organized that concert."

It wasn't a question, and he may have been right. She said she expected nothing from him. It was oddly comforting to assert that, as if he didn't exist to her the way she knew she didn't to him. He spoke about the different meanings of displacement. He refused to consider himself an exile, even if one day he would be. Outside, the bare branches of February trees looked like what he was saying, an image she might have shot once—recognizable metaphors, a formally interesting composition—but what did it really do. What was it a picture of.

That night, she told Jack about the Bangladeshi writer called Islam.

"Remember when Christian lived on the eleventh floor," Jack said.

They watched the Mets win their rubber game, a depressingly rare event, and sometimes she watched Jack and wondered if they really had a destiny with each other, and what if she left him or he left her. And what if she sent a postcard to the night-time man, like that girl. Graciously, he didn't appear in her dream, a stranger did, Islam probably, who declared, "Ecstasy is a living language." In the morning, when she spoke his name aloud, it was too big, too much. Islam had asked why she'd stopped showing her work. She didn't know, exactly, she gave him reasons, but she thought she wasn't an artist. She wasn't committed enough, she told him, and not everyone has to be an artist. That's over, that romance about being an artist. Some things were over, she acknowledged to herself.

Walking to work, she abjured scenes that had occurred years ago at one place or another, but even when a building had been complete-ly demolished, the blighted memory wasn't. Islam's questions both-ered her but she liked them, or appreciated them. In the past she'd documented many of these lost buildings; now, surprising new-old images were sprung free by involuntary processes. History pursues its psychic claims in disguise. She thought about photographing Islam, making a portrait of him. He had become entwined in what she'd renounced. First, Islam said he'd think about it, then he said no, and his refusal shut an unmarked door. She supposed she did have unwanted expectations. To appease her, probably, Islam invited her for a drink; Katherine said no. She wasn't sure what she wanted from him, or he from her, except the obvious. Katherine was suspicious in ways she hadn't been when she knew the night-time man. Maybe that was a sorry thing.

Her job involved her. She watched people carefully for unusual, even unique gestures and expressions, and listened thoughtfully. People were amazing, their stories amazed, saddened and disgusted her. Katherine was herself or wasn't during these intake interviews. She recognized a person as a site of relationships, never just an in-dividual, even when cut off from friends and family. But people felt miserably alone. Islam didn't—Katherine didn't think he did. He told her he was a beloved son, his mother's favorite, the youngest, adored by his father and brothers, and he said it with such vivacity and plea-sure, she believed him without jealousy. In the same meeting, he chided her. "You know, Katherine, you must know, I was playing you a little. I'm not really a minority, we're not a minority, you are. You have more wealth, that's all." Then he smiled brilliantly, the adored son.

Sunday, Katherine was rambling in Central Park. The night-time man's wife appeared in her path, and it wasn't a dream. She wore an unadorned black jacket, slim black pants, slingback shoes, understated make-up. Katherine admired how well-composed her image was. The wife seemed bemused, chin held high as if loftily acknowledging something or someone in the distance. A girl walked beside her, their daughter, and when they passed by, Katherine felt a furtive intimacy with her night-time rival, like a fragment secretly attached. The daughter was taller, longer-legged, unsmiling—what had happened—her face similar to her mother's, though much younger. Daughters manage fathers like him, and what do they tell themselves. What does he tell her. "I love your mother, this has nothing to do with you." What does the girl feel. The daughter's long, gold earrings danced at her swan-white neck.

Her mother's charm bracelet. Katherine saw it flutter, a golden relic hanging from a bare branch. That would be a strange picture, she thought, not easily dismissed, uncanny even. But how would she do it, if she did. Startling, what gets kept.

The Shadow of a Doubt

Imperfect knowledge accompanied him across the field to a big tent. It was strange, it was just like the tent Thomas dreamed about the night before, with green and white stripes and billowing white flaps spread wide like labia. Inside the tent, a three-piece band played "All of Me," a beguiling smell of gardenias insinuated itself, and five veiled women, their naked, fleshy bellies curling and uncurling—maybe the gypsy women from a small circus in southern Turkey—waved and pointed behind him, and there she was, Grace, his love, embracing him, lustily biting his lips. You're eating me up alive, he dream-talked, and everything was right in the world, until he awoke.

Déjà vu all over again, Thomas thought, entering the tent. His dream wasn't a flash of prognostication, he knew the ceremony and reception would be under a tent, so the dream made perfect sense, even if her marriage didn't. Its inevitability had plagued him for months, especially since Grace had once told him she couldn't be with him because she didn't know how to love, couldn't love, it wasn't him, she said, downcast, she was incapable. Hers was a hopeless, existential condition. My mother, she explained, made loving anyone impossible. Her mother had disappeared one day, didn't pick her up from kindergarten, and finally turned up dead, or was pronounced dead, it was murkily put, and that was all, she wouldn't say more, so he didn't prod Grace, assuming the disappearance was the result of another man, drugs, or alcohol. He doubted she'd died—her father kept the truth from her—but Thomas believed the terrifying, great loss and abandonment had diminished Grace's capacity to trust, and desperate insecurity carved out her being. Grace left it, and many other matters, open to interpretation; her vagueness shaped their relationship, until, disastrously bent out of shape, it disintegrated.

Now Grace was actually marrying Billy Webster, a man—Thomas would've preferred a woman—a man she could love, presumably, unless she had other motives and reasons with which she'd tie her Gordian knot. Living gardenias cascaded down thick, moss-green plastic vines, but there were no women in veils, except for Grace, when she walked down the aisle next to her father, who looked just like the New Hampshire modern-day farmer he was. This was New Hampshire, Thomas reminded himself, glancing away from Grace's swishing peau de soie dress, whose hem touched his foot as she walked toward the other man. But how much a dream tells and doesn't, how it plays tricks, just like people. His only consolation was to attend her wedding the way he would a funeral for a colleague or a former friend, because it was required and ennobled him with easy virtue.

Thomas knew only a little about Grace's dull or bright hubby who stood possessively by her side and appeared to sense subtle meanings in her every gesture, unctuous and fastidious in his affection, and grinned so broadly his eyes disappeared into folds of cheek, which looked to Thomas like abnormal growths. He's assertive, Thomas decided, a wimp, or a geek, and probably impotent. Grace's brand new husband produced CD-ROMs, a movie or two, some Broadway shows, and Thomas distrusted his dilettantism, his casualness.

Thomas prided himself on his vision and application of skill to one cause, graphic design, whose requirements called for a refined eye, precision, and creativity within limits. He served others rather than himself, far better than making art that encouraged self-indulgence. Billy Webster was a grandstander. Also, Billy Webster had once performed magic, which was how he got into theater, and read palms and handwriting. Grace had mentioned this, as if they were worthy pursuits.

She met Billy Webster after they'd split up, she explained to Thomas, when she also informed him, too delicately, as if his feelings were womanly, of their upcoming marriage. That's why she'd phoned him. It was chance, they were at a party, thrown by a close college friend she hadn't seen since, but the friend had converted to Scientology, which Grace didn't know until the party, when she heard a well-dressed group of men and women, all in their thirties, with too-bright eyes and eager, lubricious smiles, discuss E-meters and getting clear. She listened in, didn't say a word, fearing intimidation, and that's when she and Billy Webster found each other's eyes across the room. The antidisciples soon absconded from the religious or cultish party, to a bar. They talked all night. Until dawn, she'd said, and soon Billy Webster had discovered her and she him, they found each other.

—Were you lost? Thomas asked.

—Very cute.

—I am very cute. You're blind.

—He's psychic, he knows me better than I know myself.

—And that makes you happy, Thomas said, flatly.

—Yes, it does.

73

—And you can love him, Thomas said, flat-lining now.

She lost color, at least she lost color, he thought later.

—Yes, I can. I do. I'm sorry, Tommy.

He hated her saying Tommy.

—What about your mother?

—Billy let her, or he let me—he expelled her.

—Like an exorcism, Thomas joked.

—Sort of, she said. Don't laugh. It can happen.

—Accidents happen, he said.

—No, she said, Billy did it.

—You fell in love with him, I'm not a moron.

She invited him to the wedding anyway.

Thomas now hated Webster with conviction, and wished he had not been decent about making an appearance at the wedding, even though he attended more as a ghost than a person, but still, he was complying with a ritual form of masochism. He thought he hated her, he hoped so, and he strode purposefully out of the tent, to cover so much ground that the tent would disappear, as if it were his bad dream, the wedding, and Grace an aerie faerie, and Billy Webster a devil with a slimy coat, sour, steamy sweat oozing, a tiny, hairy penis, or a mouse where the phallus should have been. Thomas saw him go up in a puff of smoke. All the while he felt someone was close behind him, so he strode faster, running away, exercising his legs, but he didn't look back.

The field turned into a forest, and when Thomas reached a pond, the tent gone to a recent past, he sat upon a log near the water, heard birds singing inside the profound quiet, and dirtied the seat of his suit on the wet log with perverse pleasure. I can't go back now, he decided. Does she really believe that junk?

His twin sister, Antoinette—Tony—might. Her girlfriend's day job was as a lab technician, but she was also a working psychic, and while his twin sister wasn't in thrall or attuned to voices from beyond or the like, Tony sympathized with those who were. Because their mother thought it was all junk, the way Thomas did. Their mother was beautiful, still, very much in love with their father, who returned her love, and his twin had always felt left out. Her mother either didn't pay enough attention to her, or too much, of the bad kind, overly praised her, which sounded false to Tony, or belittled her, she said. His twin blamed their mother for everything that went wrong in her life, but he didn't. He loved her.

The last time the twins talked, over drinks, he had managed not to press a single incendiary button, steering their course through comfort zones, but then Tony said, her lips pressed against her teeth, "Mother didn't love me, she loved you because you were a boy. She's a bitch." She sat back in her chair, opening her legs wide like a muscleman on a subway car. Tony was more butch than he was. She liked sports and working out, she'd always been butch and, as a child, acted as if she believed if Thomas were nice, he would have changed his sex for her. Now he supposed he could cut off his penis and have the flesh made into a vagina with folds, but the thought made him sick. He just couldn't, he liked his penis, and, even if he did change his sex, Tony wouldn't be satisfied.

When Tony mentioned "our mother" again, Thomas absent-mindedly lifted a large plastic cup of water to his mouth, couldn't hold it somehow, and instead juggled it, kept juggling, until the cup flew into the air and doused his sister and him in spring water. Laughing, wiping herself off, she said, "If you'd soaked just me, Bro, I'd have wondered." Later, he realized his unconscious had helped him throw cold water on the conversation, a literal-minded unconscious, and kind of great.

Tony had her revenge. He left town sometime after that, and she wanted to stay in his apartment as a break from her too-attentive lover, and he said, as he opened the door to leave, Don't break anything, OK? This stuff is precious to me. He shut the door behind him, and she marched over to the refrigerator for a beer, then to the Prouvé chair he'd paid a fortune for, plopped down on it, and it crumbled beneath her. That's what she told him when he returned.

Thomas had never liked birds much, and now they were his company. He twisted around, angled his head back, sensing something standing behind him, but there was nothing. I'm thinking it, I want someone there, I'm willing it, Grace, probably, I want her. He called her name, Grace, Grace, Grace, to an indifferent forest, which regularly responded to wild breezes, not words, and then when his echo disconcerted him, her name bouncing back emptily, he concentrated on hating her, hating what he'd loved. It was better than loving and missing her, having her in absentia only. What will come now? What will happen? The future might stroke him with good fortune or lash him with lies and broken promises, all uncontrollable, like his unconscious, which allowed him to do what he wanted but couldn't in good conscience, allowed him what he feared, and safely enabled him to engage in gory scenes, loveless sex, abusive and ugly acts with his enemies and even friends. Who was a friend, anyway? Self-interest and betrayal climaxed together, satisfied bedfellows and lovers, common as dirt. He wiped the seat of his trousers without mirth.

Another love like this could shatter him, he'd crack up, go mad, or be forever changed, and he wanted that, to be out of himself, to believe ideas he absolutely never had, suddenly, and he also wished for stability and hardly any—no—he wanted no more sad surprises. He loved Grace, what a joke. What if he always loved her, what if he couldn't stop, what if he could never have what he wanted. There was too much he couldn't control. He might as well wish on a star, have his fortune read, believe in obscure pseudoscientific lore, astrology, or handwriting analysis, roll the dice, or throw a penny into this placid pond, his own Trevi Fountain. Thomas humored himself imagining farmers at the pond tossing in coins, dimes and quarters probably—the cost of wishes must be inflated, too—and if he peered in, he knew he'd see his reflection.

So, in the same, whimsical mood, he called up the myth of Narcissus. It seemed fitting, Narcissus' attachment to himself, to a reflection, all surface, though Echo loved him anyway. Her fate doomed her to repeat his words, which Narcissus might have ambivalently appreciated, since some men like to hear themselves talk and hear themselves in subservient women. Thomas, somewhat uncomfortably and almost against his will, he'd say later, looked down, but he didn't see his face. He saw the moss-covered still water, and soon, through the interstices of green slime, a woman's face floating a foot beneath the surface. Distorted, old, rotten. Disbelieving, even alarmed, he turned again, but again there was no creature behind him, and all the while the birds continued to vocalize their complaints and desires in a euphonious chorus, interrupted by a few squawks.

He stared at the rotten face, hoping to see something. It felt imperative now to realize something, to apprehend—"make it work" was his design credo. He felt, suddenly, less sure of himself than ever, but maybe there would come a sign to help him, though wishing for that made him feel more vulnerable. He stared, and occasionally a trace of his own reflection filtered through the muck, but only for a moment until the watery mirror exposed her face once more. The face changed, by the flow of water, he thought, its labile movements. And as he stared, meditating on her, or it, and this oddness, he noticed something, the thing behind him that wasn't there and the thing in front that was and yet wasn't. It wasn't clear, it was more a sensation than an idea or image. But then it became an idea: the face was Grace's dead mother's. She had, like Virginia Woolf, drowned herself, a suicide, that was why Grace couldn't love. And then: Grace's mother had been murdered, that's why her face looked hideous, she died in terror, thrown into a river. In either case, her mother was condemned to haunt the waterways of New Hampshire. So: Grace never stopped mourning her mother and hating her, too, her mother had left her, had not loved her, and how could unloved Grace love—that must be it. But Billy Webster had made Grace know her mother was gone, he let her go for Grace. No, he told her that her mother had been kidnapped, that's what Webster insisted, and she had never wanted to leave Grace, and she believed him.

Why couldn't he have calmed her? Led her from doubt? Why couldn't he have given her what she needed? Thomas couldn't accept his fate, either, to have lost her. He wasn't her knight in shining armor.

It's not your fault, a voice whispered.

Thomas shifted around, and a form lay on the forest floor, like a woman's, a shadow, or a ghost, then of a man, a child, a woman again, but there, absolutely, it was. It appeared to be wearing a hat, with a feather, as when an Indian stood in his doorway when he was a child, and, though Thomas awoke, the Indian stayed there for several minutes, he wore an elaborate feather headdress, his bare chest smooth and brown, luminous in the dark of the bedroom.

Now she, he, or it sat up.

The indecipherable shadow muttered: Thomas, Thomas, don't be silly.

That's what it sounded like, he thought, he heard that, but do ghosts or sibyls call you silly? He was hearing things, of course, hearing what he wanted. Thomas believed the ghostlike shape was created by a weave of branches and leaves, the winds causing it to shift its shape. It was a shadow created by nature, the play of elements, and maybe of his desire, with an illusion of physicality, but even when he shut his eyes, then quickly opened them, it was there. He accepted his own explanations or interpretations and waited for more.

Someone will love you, the voice said in a deeper register.

Thomas scoffed, then he snorted, and the birds stopped singing, as if they recognized his sounds as derisive and objected with their silence. He stood up, brushed off his pants, boldly walked toward the form, and stuck his arm through the air above it. The shadow disappeared and his own shape hovered, instead. Selective hearing, selective memory, selective living. Maybe he was going mad, this was it, but he didn't feel mad. Would he ever be happy? He couldn't imagine it. A dream is a disguise, his college therapist explained, while his Spanish teacher taught Calderón's La vida es sueño, and if a dream is

79

a disguise, and life is a dream, then life is a disguise, too. The tautology satisfied him since it demonstrated he was able to think, so he wasn't crazy yet, but if life were a disguise, what did it disguise. Was there a design? No, not a design, there was too much randomness, but then what does life disguise?

Thomas sat on the log again, thoroughly engaged in the question, listening to his thoughts, to the birds who sang again or argued or cried, until he fell asleep. He must have fallen asleep, because time passed and kept passing, and reality didn't feel real, he was looking at himself looking at himself. The big striped tent was back, he saw himself go through the opening, he saw her walk down the aisle, everything repeated itself, he saw himself, he saw his twin, Tony, she was a man and a woman, and she didn't hate him, his parents smiled, then looked sadly upon him. He saw life rushing by, was he dead? Life is a dream, life is a dream. Now everyone was in disguise, everyone, and he fled the tent again, horrified, because if everyone's in disguise, and a disguise is also disguise, then where does it end. IN DEATH. In death, in death. He was dead. He wasn't asleep, he was dead. Life disguises death. We only think we're alive. That was the Tibetan Book of the Dead, and, realizing that, he breathed. He wasn't dead, he was only reading a book. Nothing made sense. A dream is life, life is death, death is life, and all of it is a disguise. Everything. Lies, lies upon lies, only lies on lies only. He finished running away and again he was where he was, by the pond, and the birds were singing, and a mourning dove flew to him and alighted on his chest, so, startled, he rubbed his eyes to better see the beautiful grey bird.

The mourning dove chirped: The biggest lies are the ones you tell yourself.

OK, that's good, Thomas said to the talking bird.

It was as if I'd seen a ghost, but I was the ghost, he explained to his friends later. He told his twin, Tony, that he knew she was a man and a woman, and he thought, in his dream, he was also. Tony liked him better then, maybe forever after. Thomas did forget Grace, he forgot Billy Webster, and one day he forgot falling asleep and dreaming at the pond, because that's what he'd told himself. It was all a dream, life is a dream, a dream is life, life disguises death, and only I can lie to myself.

Lunacies

The first astronaut to reach the Moon proclaimed: "One small step for man, one giant leap for mankind." Neil Armstrong, his head entombed in a white bubble, his eyes obliterated by Moon-resilient plastic, gravityless in a bloated space suit, planted the U.S. flag right where he stood.

Later, Armstrong realized his mistake. He was supposed to have said: "One small step for *a* man, one giant leap for mankind."

"As you read this, the Moon is moving away from the Earth. Each year the Moon steals some of Earth's rotational energy and uses it to propel itself about 3.8 centimeters higher in its orbit."

He had never encountered a parasite he didn't, in some way, envy for a kind of perverse talent.

"The tidal forces of the Moon—and the Sun—don't act only on the oceans, they act on the land too. Stand on the equator, and the land beneath you will rise and fall as much as twenty-one inches over the course of twenty-four hours."

Vertigo restrained her from standing near expansive plate-glass windows on the upper floors of top-heavy skyscrapers. She teetered on high heels, the foundation undulating beneath her feet, or maybe she was moonstruck again.

"The Moon is about the same age as Earth. When the Moon was created, it was much closer to Earth and appeared ten times larger in the sky."

In Sunday school, he asked his teacher, "Why did God make the Moon without people?" His father told him the moon was too cold for people, it was the dark side of God's work; then his mother broke in, "Your father's being funny. Look at the TV. Michael Jackson, honey, he's moon-walking."

"The Moon is full when the Earth is between the Sun and Moon, it is a New Moon when the Moon is between the Sun and the Earth."

Nocturnal creatures, cats nightly play and prance, hunting mice, hearing their faint movements behind plaster walls, while their owners beseech moon gods for love and power.

"The Moon is not a planet, but a satellite of the Earth."

Being an identical twin was way cooler than being a virtual one—adopted at the same time, same age, but studies showed virtuals were very different people. He and his brother were unique, even if they looked the same, and he didn't moon about his lost individuality, the way his twin did.

"An afterglow—also called post-luminescence—is a wide arc of glowing light that can sometimes be seen high in the western sky at twilight; it is caused by fine particles of dust scattering light in the upper atmosphere."

She loved the line, "When a pickpocket meets a saint, he sees only his pockets." She scratched his right arm and nudged him. "Naked, you don't have pockets," he said, "unless you're a fucking kangaroo." Moonlight did nothing for this guy.

"Alan Shepard, when he was on the Moon, hit a golf ball and drove it 2400 feet, nearly half a mile."

The moon is made of green cheese, and that crater on it, it's really a man in the moon. And I haven't drunk any moonshine.

"At the full Moon, the times of moonrise and moonset have advanced so that the Moon rises about the same time the Sun sets, and the Moon sets about the same time the sun rises."

Their honeymoon, after years of living together, still scared up traditional illusions, intimations of ecstasy, a time out from reality, and when the second night of connubial bliss yawned on, she quoted George Meredith, "Where may these lunatics have gone to spend the Moon."

"Ramadan begins with the sighting of the new crescent Moon in the ninth month of the lunar calendar. But whose sighting counts?"

She read the first sentence of the book: "A white dog bayed at the Moon, a true moon-dog, with moon-blindness, more blind sometimes than others." The writer must be a lunatic.

"Dr. Eugene Shoemaker, a geological surveyor who educated the Apollo mission astronauts about craters, never made it to the Moon... He was rejected as an astronaut because of medical problems. After he died, his ashes were placed on board the Lunar Prospector spacecraft on January 6, 1999... and fulfilled Dr. Shoemaker's last wish."

Once in a blue moon, the tides pull at us. They invoke humans to recall primitive ancestors who shouted at the sky, noise-makers who yowled in the dark, beckoning forces and spirits to aid their survival. Now, domesticated dogs guard their masters' lives, and house cats daydream about orangutans swinging happily from branch to branch. Human beings cannot stop being afraid of the dark or imagining complete freedom.

The Way We Are

I walked over to the café on a sunny and boring Thursday afternoon in Amsterdam. I found him sitting at the bar, next to a young blond woman and an older man. Their heads were inclined toward each others' at an angle that indicated drunkenness.

"Let's go to a movie." They all looked up. "Come on," I said to him, "I'm going nuts in this town. I'll pay."

"What do you want to see?" he asked.

"*The Way We Were*, Streisand and Redford. I want to cry."

"Shit," he said and slid off the barstool, leaving the woman and man. He didn't say goodbye. They watched us go.

We jumped into a taxi at the Rembrandtplein and sped to the cinema as if leaving the scene of a crime. There was some relief just being in a taxi. We arrived at the movie two minutes before showtime. "You see," I muttered to him, "we were meant to be here."

Four o'clock in the afternoon and there were only twenty people in the theater—tourists or depressives at this time of day. We took seats in the center of the hall. There was no one in front of us. I slipped my feet out of my shoes, and he went to take a piss. He'd had eight beers by the time I'd commandeered him out of the café. He returned with chocolates.

It was a lowdown, dirty day. I was leading the life of a bat, a fascinated bat, in a dark hole, eating candy and gobbling images. I plugged my naked feet in between the empty seats as tears rolled down my cheeks. I've learned to cry silently during movies. The usher, who was probably bored, too, wanting to be outside, not here with us on a sunny day, asked me to remove my feet from the seat in front. I did as I was told, my eyes on the screen, but my friend immediately threw his legs over the seat in front of him. He looked with menace at the usher. The usher took note and left.

Redford's telling Streisand why she's not right for him just as the usher returns. My friend says he won't take his feet down. The usher stands there. My friend pretends he is absorbed in what's on the screen. A minute or two passes. They're in a standoff. I'm trying to watch the movie. Streisand and Redford are fighting. Then fists start flying. Streisand is crying. With one eye on the screen, I try to break up the fight between the two incensed men. My friend turns and yells at me, "Why are you on his side?" "I'm not, I'm not," I protest. His glasses fly off so I drop to the floor, crying, to search for them.

They're swinging at each other and I'm on the floor wondering what's happening to Streisand and Redford. The usher pulls away from my friend, who had him in a bear hug. The usher shouts "Politie" and starts up the aisle; my friend storms up the aisle after him. I try to concentrate on the movie. Someone else finds my friend's glasses—no one is really able to watch the movie—and when he returns he puts them on and says, "I'm demanding our money back."

We walk to the lobby where he threatens the ticket taker, an overweight elderly woman. He looms over her, all hair and eyes. "Let's go," I say sensibly, "the cops will be here any minute."

Back on the street, on the outside, he throws his arm around me and curses. He murmurs that the world is too hard for us. We walk a block or two and begin to cross a busy street when he pushes me forward, toward an oncoming car, insisting it should stop. The car swerves. We are on the white line, rush-hour traffic running both ways.

"They should stop," my friend says. He seizes my hand. This time we both jump into the path of an oncoming car. He kicks it because it doesn't stop. He is wearing sandals. He kicks it a second time; the third time he dents it. The car stops and the driver bounces out. He asks, in Dutch, "What the hell is going on?" My friend responds, in English, "We had the right of way." My friend blames the driver, who is both furious and incredulous. Then we walk away.

We are trailed by the car driver, a taxi driver who had witnessed every-thing, and a man on a bicycle, another eyewitness. We arrive at a bridge, leading these three like pied pipers. My friend urges me, a foreigner, to flee, to run away. "Go," he says, "before the cops get here."

I march to the corner and stand behind a telephone pole. I watch my friend, the car driver, the taxi driver, the bicyclist, and the cops who arrive in no time. They all talk for a while. Then my friend is escorted into the cop car where he disappears in the backseat.

The cop car drives away, followed by the three indignant Dutch men. I telephone someone and explain that my friend has been taken away. Someone reassures me that he will be released immediately because this is Amsterdam.

I walk home. I avoid the movie house. My friend is not charged. His behavior, he tells me, is considered *ludieke*, too strange, really, to be a crime.

A Greek Story

A friend announced that what she was going to tell me was the best thing she'd ever done. It was her best story.

She and her friend were about to start traveling in Greece. On the first day they were in Athens, where my friend lives, she stepped on her very nearsighted friend's glasses. The nearsighted friend insisted anyway on being the driver of the car they rented. The nearsighted one pasted a piece of paper over the shattered lens and off they drove. The nearsighted friend drove everywhere. But they contacted another friend in the States, to send a new pair of glasses as soon as possible.

Everywhere they went the nearsighted friend saw out of one eye only. Maybe this is why, when they arrived at Mesalongi, where Lord Byron witnessed the massive battle against the Turks, she especially found the local population menacing.

Then finally it was time for the nearsighted friend to go home, to the States. By now, at some poste restante in Greece, they discovered that a FedEx package was waiting, with the nearsighted friend's new glasses. A note told them that the package was being held in the customs building at the international airport, from which the nearsighted one would fly home.

On the day she was to leave, they went to that building. It was very hard to find the door to enter it, it was a very large, impersonal, and opaque-looking building, and for a long time they couldn't find its entrance. When they did, finally, my friend, who speaks Greek, asked an official the whereabouts of her friend's package. They were directed to a series of rooms, and, in each room, hundreds of packages, some marked Urgent, were strewn on many tables. Many of the cartons and large envelopes were broken or torn. In about half an hour, though, my friend miraculously spied the Fed Ex envelope, with the glasses. But at the door was a customs official who informed them, in Greek, that there was duty to pay on the contents. A lot of duty.

At first calm, my friend explained that her nearsighted friend was leaving for the States that very day and wouldn't even be bringing the new glasses into Greece. The customs official said that it didn't matter and repeated that there was duty to pay and she had to pay it. My friend became agitated and also repeated the same thing: the contents were her friend's personal property, which she wasn't even bringing into Greece and she was leaving that day. Nothing had any effect upon the customs official. He continued to say money was owed, and it had to be paid. Then, my friend told me, she launched into Greek anger, that's how she explained it, which naturally made me think about Greek tragedy.

My friend began cursing and shouting in Greek, a torrent of words. All the while the nearsighted friend listened but didn't understand. My friend shouted and shouted and then, as she shouted, she surreptitiously opened the FedEx envelope, removed the eyeglass case, and took the glasses from it. Then still shouting vehemently in Greek, she returned the case to the envelope, closed it, threw the envelope on the table in front of the customs official, took her nearsighted friend by the hand, and stormed out. When the two had gone through the door, my friend took the glasses from her pocket, gave them to her friend, explained what she'd done, and said, run.

After my friend told me the story, I reminded her how she began it, by saying it was the best thing she had ever done. Oh, she said, that's awful if it's true.

The Recipe

—Sadness, that's normal, it goes with the territory, but becoming bitter, bitterness is to be avoided, he said.

—Be a saint instead, she said.

Instead, he'd live from the largesse of a common madness, not just his own, not just from his sadness, he'd lament and move on, lament and move on.

My lament, can't do it, my way.

Clay wouldn't ever want to relinquish internal rhyme, rhyming was a mnemonic device, too, and venerable for a reason, and, along with that, he relied on the beautiful histories meshed inside the roots of words.

—We don't determine what words mean, they determine what we mean, Clay said, later. We don't determine much.

Cornelia was a film editor and also translated documents and titles for a movie company, she also plied her insightful eye as a photo researcher and archivist for a wealthy eccentric, who never left his house and liked to know what was going on, but only in pictures. The eccentric hated to read.

—It would be great if pictures told a story, Cornelia said, but they don't. They tell too many, or they don't tell any.

—Words, also, he said.

—Images are easier to misread, she said.

—I don't know.

Subtitles crowded the image, she explained more than once, they changed the picture, even dominated it, and besides, reading words on a screen disrupted the cinematic flow. He wasn't sure that was all bad, but then he was suspicious of images, which he didn't make. He was wary of words, too, which he used and tried to remake, so he had reason for anxiety. In her business, they talked about "getting a read on" a script, on meaning, sort of instantaneously.

A place for words, orphaned, wayward, no words,
no images, what then.

The lovers argued about the small things, about cleaning up after themselves in their apartment, as responsible adults do, supposedly, and petty problems, at work and with relative strangers, and also the large things, love, politics, history, friendship, art, poetry, which he wrote, when inevitably inconsiderate matter that had earlier settled in words and sentences extruded layers of their pasts, lived together and separately.

Code, just for now, when you mean its opposite,
bright lust of sullen night.

He'd been stunned by an obituary: "To my dear friends and chums, It has been wonderful and at times it had been grand and for me, now, it has been enough." The man—it was signed "Michael"—

96

had had the presence of mind to write and place his own death notice, it resonated a unique thoughtfulness, sad and mad, was he a suicide? And, on TV, a Fuji commercial declaimed a new longing for the fast-escaping present: "Because life won't stay still while you go home and get your camera."

Writing death, perpetual, language like a
house, an asylum, an orphanage. In a dream I
wasn't, argued with someone or myself, so lost.
Perpetual death of words, writing.

He wasn't his dream's hero, but there are no heroes, just cops. Clay stopped to watch two beat cops, surreptitiously he hoped, while they canvassed the street for errant civilians, ordinary or unusual, and the cops, they're ordinary and they're not, and out of uniform they're nothing, or they're nothing just like him, dumb mortals compelled by ignorant, invisible forces, which happened to be, in their case, part of the job. A police car sped by, like a siren, in time or too late to stop it, the robbery, murder, the robber, murderer. He asked the butcher for stew meat but studied another butcher at the bloodstained chopping block who expertly sliced off a layer of fat, thick and marbled, from a porterhouse. Fat enriches the meat's taste, his mother taught him, and also she warned, it's better to be dead and buried than frank and honest. She said she knew things he didn't that she hoped he'd never know, it was the part of her past she wouldn't tell him.

—At the end of the day, everyone wants someone to cook for them, a woman, who was probably waiting for the porterhouse, announced to a man by her side.

The man appeared to understand and nodded his head. Clay wondered if giving the appearance of understanding was actually understanding, in some sense, and if duplicity of this sort was necessary for a society's existence, maybe even at its basis or center, and not the ancient totem Émile Durkheim theorized. People regularly don't understand each other, but if that were constantly apparent, rather than gestures of tacit agreement and recognition, a stasis, punctuated by violent acts everywhere, would stall everyone for eternity.

"Security has now been doubled at the stadium, but people's enjoyment won't be hampered, officials say." The radio announcer's voice sounded out of place in the warm, yeasty bakery, where he now was, doing errands like a responsible mate. The baker tuned the radio to a station that gave bulletins every few minutes, which some people listened to all day long, so they knew the news word by word, and Clay imagined they could recite it like a poem.

An epic, way to remember. A gesture, song, war,
a homecoming. Fighting writing my death,
persistent oxymoron. Perpetrator. Victim.
Terror to fight terror. Fire or an argument with
fire. Firefight. Spitfire. Lawless, Eliot Ness,
childhood. Fighting against or for terror, lies
in mouth. Can't leave home without it. Get a
horse instead.

People expected the unexpected, unnatural and natural disasters, a jet crashing in the ocean, all lost, hurricanes beating down towns, all lost, bombs doing their dirty work, lives lost and shattered, houses destroyed, and attentive listeners needed to know, instantly, for a sense of control or protection, and for the inevitable shock of recognition: I'm still alive.

The baker's son Joey, dressed in white like a surgeon, the skin on his florid cheeks dusted with flour, asked him what he wanted, then bantered with him as he always did.

—Sun, Clay, ever see it? You're pasty-faced.

—You're flour-faced. I want a sourdough loaf, and the recipe.

—Forget about it, Joey the baker's son said. Family secret for five generations.

—I'll get it.

—You're just like your mother, Joey said.

His mother had played the violin, and when he couldn't sleep at night, to quiet him after a bad dream, she'd stand in the doorway to his bedroom and pluck each string with adoring concentration. A lullaby, maybe, some song that consoled him for having to leave consciousness at all. He was attached to her concentration, like the strings to her instrument, and this specific image of her, mother violinist bent and absorbed, resisted passing time's arbitrariness, its uneven dissipations. Her face, for a long time now, rested only against walls or stood upright on tables in framed photographs, and he scarcely remembered a conversation they had, just a sentence or two.

Here, waiting. Can't leave home, without a
horse. Get a read on. Long ago, here, a drama
with teeth, reneging, nagging. Cracked plates,
baseball bats, stains on home room floor, same
as before, stains like Shroud of Turin.

Jesus bled, writing death, fighting terror.

He hadn't moved away from the old neighborhood, waiting for something, teaching English and American literature at the high school he attended, while he grew older in the same place, without stopping time, though he found his illusions encouraged and indemnified by traces of the past, like the indentations in the gym's floor, and, more than traces, bodies, like the baker's and the butcher's, and their children, who would replace them, and stand in their places, in a continuity Clay wouldn't keep up, even by staying in the neighborhood.

Cornelia believed the cult around the Shroud of Turin demonstrated that people do appreciate abstraction, an image instead of a body, though it wasn't exactly an abstraction but close enough. Even if the cloth had once rested on a body, theirs was a reverence for an impression, drawn from but not the same as the body—even if the body wasn't Christ's, since scientists carbon-dated the cloth much later than his death. The cloth was just matter, material separate from and attached to history.

Not the thing, the stain, palimpsest of pain.
Life served with death a sanction.

Sometimes Joey the baker's son let him go into the back of the store to watch other white-coated men knead dough, their faces also dusted in white, their concentration, like his mother's on her violin, complete, and he viewed them as content, absorbed in good work. Their hands knew exactly how much to slap and pound, when to stop—every movement was essential. Then Clay ruminated, the way he always did in the bakery, about being a baker; in the butcher shop, he thought about being a butcher. He wanted to be like Joey, they'd gone to school together. If he were, he'd know simple limits, why an action was right or wrong, because the consequences would be immediate, and as usual he rebuked himself for romanticizing their labor and imagining an idyllic life for, say, the old baker and the baker's son he'd known since he was a child, with a life better than his, because, he told Cornelia that night, their work was what it was, nothing else, its routine might be comforting, his wasn't. In the moment, as he watched their hands and smelled baking bread's inimitable aroma, he also felt that the bakers dwelled, as he did, in fantasy, that it enveloped them daily, and that what they did might be something else for them, too. Joey thought he was funny, but Clay loved the way Joey treated him, he felt Joey appreciated him in ways no one else did.

—The butcher, the baker, the candlestick maker, Cornelia teased.

—Cut it out, Clay said.

—Your heroes might surprise you someday, she said.

—I'd like that, Clay said.

—I bet you wouldn't, Cornelia said.

He told her about a distressed woman in the news who had found out she'd been adopted when she was twenty-one, which made sense to her, she was even glad, because she had never felt close to her parents, who were like aliens to her, and then the woman spent years searching for her birth parents. When she was fifty, she found her mother, who'd given her up for adoption because she'd been unmarried and only fifteen. But the mother she unearthed wasn't the mother she expected or wanted, so the woman was very disappointed. Also, her birth father was disreputable and long dead.

—Do you think people have the right to know? Clay asked.

—A constitutional right, Cornelia said.

—Okay.

—What about the right to privacy?

—Maybe some rights kill others.

If Clay turned violent, deranged, on the street, the cops would subdue and cuff him, take him in, interrogate him, or they might just shoot him on the spot, if he charged them menacingly, resisted them, or appeared to be carrying. The cops waited to arrest him and others from doing things they didn't know they could do or felt they had to do or did because inside them lurked instinctual monsters. He didn't know what he had in him, but he knew restraint, and he recognized, as Max Weber wrote early in the twentieth century, that only the state had the right to kill, no one else, and that fact alone defined the state. But where he lived everyone had the right to bear arms, to answer and resist the state's monopoly on power. That was the original idea, anyway, but if Clay carried a gun, he might use it, because he didn't know what he had in him.

Better to be dead and buried than frank and honest, his mother had said. His father ghosted their dining room table, his tales gone to the grave with him and now to his wife's grave also. One night his father hadn't come home from work the way he always did, Clay was seven, and his mother's face never regained its usual smile. She smiled, but not the way she once had. When little Clay walked into the butcher shop or the bakery, he felt the white-clothed men looking sympathetically at him, prying into him for feelings he hadn't yet experienced. The fatherly baker gave him an extra cookie or two, and in school, even on the baseball field, Joey the baker's son didn't call him names anymore, even when he struck out. But his mother clutched his little hand more tightly on the streets, and he learned there was something to fear about just being alive. He learned his father was dead, but it didn't mean much to him, death didn't then, and soon it became everything.

—It's why you're a depressive, Cornelia said. Losing a parent at that age.

—I guess, he said.

—It's why you hold on to everything.

Clay didn't throw out much, like matchbooks and coasters from old restaurants and bars that had closed, outdated business cards, and with this ephemera he first kept his father with him. There was dust at the back of his father's big desk that he let stay there. There was hair in his father's comb, which had been pushed to the back of the bathroom cabinet, so Clay collected the evidence in an envelope, and wondered later if he should have the DNA tested. What if his father wasn't his father? Maybe there was someone alive out there for him, a father, but his mother disabused him of the possibility, and played the violin so consolingly that Morpheus himself bothered to carry him off to a better life. Now, scratches on a mahogany table that once nestled close to his father's side of the bed and his mother's yellowing music books, her sewing cushion with its needles tidily stuck where she'd pushed them last, marked matter-of-fact episodes and incidents in their lives, when accidents occurred or things happened haphazardly, causing nicks and dents, before death recast them as shrines.

How long has this scrap been in the corner of a bureau drawer, he might ask himself, did it have a history. He could read clues incorrectly, though it didn't matter to him if his interpretations were wrong, because there was no way to know, and it wasn't a crime, he wasn't killing anyone. Cornelia's habits were different, heuristically trained and developed in the editing room, where she let go of dialogue and images, thousands of words and pictures every day, where she abandoned, shaped, or controlled objects more than he felt he could, ever.

At last. To last. Last remains. What lasts
remains. What, last. Shroud of Turin, Torino
mio, home to Primo, Levi knew the shroud.

In Clay's sophomore English classes, in which the students read George Eliot's *The Mill on the Floss* and Edith Wharton's *Ethan Frome*, his charges contested the rules for punctuation and grammar and argued for spellings and neologisms they used on the Internet and in text messaging. They preferred shorthand, acronyms, to regular English, they wanted speed. He argued for communication, commonality, and clarity, the three C's, for knowing rules and then breaking them consciously, even conscientiously. He attempted to engage them, as he was engaged, in the beauties and mysteries of the history that lives in all languages. It's present, it's still available, he'd say. And, by tracing the root of a word to its origin in Latin, Greek, or Sanskrit, and then by delving into its etymology, they could find how meanings had shifted over the years through usage. A few students caught his fervor, he thought, and who knew what would happen to them as they grew up, maybe they'd discover that love, that attachment. Curiously, there were many more new words each year, an explosion added to recent editions of dictionaries, more proportionately than had previously entered editions of the tomes he revered, and yet he remembered, always, what the words once meant, their first meanings. Cornelia told him it was another way he hung on to the past, and grammar countered his internal mess.

The problem is proportion, Clay thought, how to live proportionately. He passed the bakery on his way home, maybe he'd buy cinnamon buns for him and Cornelia for breakfast, and with an image of the pastries and her at the table, so that he could already taste morning in his mouth, he entered the store. It was busy as usual, and Clay waited on line, listening for the casual banter of the bakers, and when he drew nearer to the long counter, he overheard Joey the baker's son.

—I'd kill all of them, nuke 'em, torture's too good for them.

Clay continued to wait, suspended in place, breathing in the bakery's perfume, when finally he reached the front of the line, where the baker's son smiled warmly, the way he always did.

—I got you the recipe, you pasty-faced poet, Joey said.

He always teased him, ever since they were kids. Clay thanked him, smiled, and asked for two cinnamon buns, and then Joey handed him the famous recipe for sourdough bread, which in their family's version was littered with salty olive pieces. The cinnamon buns were still hot, fragrant. Fresh, Clay thought, fresh is a hard word to use, fresh or refreshed. There were suggestions, associations, and connotations always to words, he should stress this more to his students, because the connotations of a word often meant as much as its denotation, sometimes more, and there was ambiguity, ambiguity thrives, because words were the same as life.

Traces, stains, call it noir, in the shadows,
torture for us. And the child, the hooded
childhood. Fresh ambiguity to contradict
contradictions, refresh
what remains somewhere else.

The beat cops stationed themselves on the same corner, at the same time, so in a way they made themselves targets or spectacles, Clay thought, or even, by their presence, drew enraged, desperate civilians to them, like a recipe for disaster.

Walking home, mostly oblivious to the familiar streets, Clay looked over the ingredients. A teaspoon of balsamic vinegar, that may have been the secret the baker's family treasured for generations. Or the molasses and tablespoon of rum, that might have been their innovation. Cornelia wasn't in the apartment when he arrived home, she was the one who wanted the recipe, and the rooms felt emptier than usual.

He boiled water, brewed tea, opened the newspaper, couldn't look at the pictures or read the words, stared at the cabinets, they needed fresh paint. He'd cook tonight, a beef stew, because at the end of the day, he remembered the woman saying, everyone wants someone to cook for them. He stood up and, without really thinking, opened a kitchen drawer and tossed the recipe in the back.

Later

Marvin paused at the entrance of the Dakota. He scanned it and willed himself on. A stout, white doorman saluted, Good afternoon, Mr. Gaye, go right in, Mr. Lennon is expecting you, and Marvin faded into the recesses of the legendary building. "Mama, there's too many of you crying," the doorman awkwardly sang.

In a plush elevator, sort of a confessional, Marvin sank onto a banquette. *Rosemary's Baby* was heavy, he thought. The legs that appeared to start at his waist felt useless. He stroked the velvet cushion beneath him. Sweet.

John jumped up from the grand, making a picture with those wire shades and babydoll smile. "Hey, Marvin, what's going on?" Ironic but it's cool. John has dug Marvin forever, before "Let's Get It On," maybe after hearing "Can I Get A Witness?" *I love too hard, my friends sometime say, but I believe, I believe, that a woman should be loved that way, Can I get a witness.* Marvin Gaye was out of John's reach in 1963. *Witness, witness.* Then the Fab Four arrived in New York for the *Ed Sullivan Show.* John phoned into Murray the K's radio show. "Hey, Marvin, did you know—I asked him to play 'Pride and Joy.'" John sings, "Pride and joy, baby boy, pride and joy, telling the world, you're my pride and joy." Marvin's embarrassed.

It's 1979, and Marvin has tumbled into his dark ages, spiritually, he'd say; psychologically, John'd say. Marvin tells John: "I'm splitting to London, I'm all played out, this business is killing me." He also hears himself admit: "I don't know about the duets, John. I'm fucked up." Marvin can usually open up some to John, something about their backgrounds, even the primal scream thing. We all have our demons. *Mother, you had me, but I never had you. Mama don't go.*

Marvin's talking but can't get Jackie Wilson to leave his head. You never know, you're on top, and then zero. Last week Marvin visited a hole in the ground, the rest home where Jackie, Mr. Excitement, lay in a vegetative state. Withering, shrinking, ugly. Jackie shouldn't be ugly. The listless attendant told Marvin that Jackie couldn't hear anything, but Marvin sang to him, anyway.

John's hippie-dippy male secretary hands Marvin a mug of tea, sweet and dark. Ain't this the life, white grand, white couch. Marvin kicks back, the weed relaxing him. Jackie was singing his hit "Lonely Teardrops" when he collapsed, Dick Clark saw Jackie drop, and hit his head real hard on the stage, and that was it—over, man—in a coma almost five years. Jackie danced like a boxer, like Joe Louis, man, he could move. "In the place I was after Tammi died. I didn't want to sing, I couldn't."

"You and she weren't...." John says.

"It wasn't like that." Marvin watches something behind John. "She was young and good, so good."

"I'm no Tammi Terrell," John says.

"Man, you're so right, 'woman is the maker of the world.'" John laughs and tells Marvin he wants to find a groove, a straight-ahead sound, round up the best sideman, a top rhythm section, with a bass player like James Jamerson (Marvin knows there's no-one like him around, either), and turn a lyric like "Love is wanting to be loved" funky. Real, on the money, no bullshit. John's tired of the bullshit. His cover of Ben E. King's "Stand by Me" was pathetic, but Marvin doesn't say it. He doesn't say he's dying for the kind of respect John gets. Marvin starts to croon, "Lonely teardrops, lonely teardrops," and his palms tap his thighs. He stands, John walks to the piano, Marvin follows, swaying a little. "Come home, come home, just say you will, my heart is fine, just give me another chance for our romance, every day you've been away you know my heart does nothing but burn." John reaches for the lines, Marvin's already there.

Collaborating puts you through a lot of intense shit. They both know that. Marvin was once married to Berry Gordy's sister. He thinks Yoko and she could be twins. "That was heavy, my boss's sister is my wife for seventeen years, it's like you with Paul, it didn't go down great around Motown," Marvin says.

"Imagine" was soulful, Marvin tells him, not funky but soulful. John shoots him a familiar half-smile, half-frown, and Marvin sits beside him at the piano. John slides over. Marvin looks at the keys and begins noodling "Imagine," but his left hand belongs to Ray Charles. John returns to his mother Julia, the familiar refrain. "Yoko is actually more like my mum, don't laugh, she's no nonsense, like Julia. Yoko took me back after I'd been a foolish lad. I really hurt her. Julia would've always been there if she could."

Marvin shakes his head affirmatively and sings, "Imagine there's no heaven, it's easy if you try, imagine all the people living for today, imagine there's no country, it isn't hard to do, nothing to kill or die for, and no religion too, imagine all the people living life in peace…"

John could never have written it without Yoko. He cocks his head and, like a chorus of one, talk-sings: "Father, father, we don't need to escalate, war is not the answer… You know, we've got to find a way to bring some loving here today… Don't punish me with brutality, talk to me, so you can see, what's going on." They're trading lines, then blending them contrapuntally.

What's going on. Marvin can't go home, shouldn't, he's escaping to London, but his mother needs him here, his children, too, and he can't make it, he has to save himself from the madness, his madness. He doesn't know what else to do. He's weirdly determined to give something to John, their bond is new, maybe peculiar, ain't that peculiar, but he wants to leave him with promise, a song they can do. It'll be about hope and home, motherless and fatherless children. It's more for him than for John, probably. John stands, singing the line "Don't punish me with brutality" over and over. "Imagine" and "What's Going On" are talking to each other. Marvin pumps the pedals, his left hand striding, his right bridging more than songs now, and he looks up at John. That intent face has crumpled, sort of, but he's content, maybe. Marvin intones, "Nothing to kill or die for," while John chants, "Don't punish me, don't punish me." That's it, Marvin thinks. It's a beginning.

More weed and lines of coke. Marvin tells John they'll go to the studio, get a version of it down, they've got their idea, a duet of two minds, voices, old songs into new. Dynamite. It can work, and they're both wired. Marvin hears himself saying again, "I'm fucked up now. We'll get it down, when I'm back in the States." Imagine. The sun is coming up over Central Park. Marvin pulls on his coat. "It's a promise, man."

"I'll be here," John says. "Later."

Love Sentence

O, know, sweet love, I always write of you, / And you and love are still my argument; / So all my best is dressing old words new, / Spending again what is already spent; / For as the sun is daily new and old, / So is my love still telling what is told.
—William Shakespeare, Sonnet 76

Evelina lowered her lids while he read. It was a very beautiful evening, and Ann Eliza thought afterward how different life might have been with a companion who read poetry like Mr. Ramy.
—Edith Wharton, *Bunner Sisters*

It's strange… it's strange! / His words are carved in my heart. / Would real love be a misfortune for me?
—Verdi, *La Traviata*

I wrote and told you everything, Felice, that came into my mind at the time of writing. It is not everything, yet with some perception one can sense almost everything… I don't doubt that you believe me, for if I did you would not be the one I love, and nothing would be free of doubt.
—Franz Kafka, to Felice Bauer, July 13, 1913.

Everything Paige thought about love, anything she felt about love, was inadequate and wrong. It didn't matter to her that in some way, from some point of view, someone couldn't actually be wrong about an inchoate thing like love. "An inchoate thing like love" is feeble language. If my language is feeble, Paige thought, isn't my love?

Love, are you feeble?

It was spring, and in the spring a young man's, a young woman's, heart turned heedlessly, helplessly, heartlessly, to love. Were those hearts skipping beats? Were eager suitors walking along broad avenues hoping beyond hope that at the next turn the love they had waited for all their lives would notice them and halt midstep or midsentence, dumbstruck, love struck? Were women and men, women and women, men and men, late at night, sitting in dark bars, surrounded by smoky glass mirrors, pledging their minds and bodies?

In her mind's eye, Paige could see the lovers in a bar, where plaintive Chet Baker was singing, "They're writing songs of love, but not for me," and Etta James wailing, "You smiled and then the spell was cast… For you are mine at last." And what did the lovers sing to each other? Did they, would they, utter the words I love you? On the computer screen, "I love you" winked impishly at Paige.

I love you.

Paige wondered whether words of love, love talk, would survive, whether that courtly diction would rest easy on the computer screen, where words appeared easily, complacent and indifferent, and disappeared more casually, deleted or scrolled into nothing or into the memory of a machine, and so wouldn't the form dictate the terms, ultimately? Wouldn't love simply vanish?

Even so, I love you.

Once upon a time the impassioned word was scratched into dirt, smeared and slapped onto rough walls, carved into trees, chiseled into stone, impressed onto paper, then printed into books. On paper, in books, the words waited patiently and were handy, always visible, evidence of love. In that vague, formative past, love was written with a flourish, and it flourished.

Is the computer screen an illuminated manuscript, evanescent, impermanent, but with a memory that is no longer mine or yours? Is love a memory that is never mine, never yours?

Remember I love you.

Paige thought, I give my memory to this machine. I want ecstasy, not evidence. Can a machine's remembering prove anything about love? If she points to its glowing face, could Paige attest, as one might of a poem written on the finest ivory linen paper: Here, this is evidence of my love.

> "For you are so entirely fair, / To love a part, injustice were/… But I love all, and every part, and nothing less can ease my heart." (Sir Charles Sedley)

Paige glanced at the little marks, letters in regular patterns making words and paragraphs, covering sheets of paper that were spread haphazardly around her on the desk and on the floor, and she gazed at the computer's face, as comforting and imperturbable as a TV screen.

Love, my enemy, even now I love you.

Romantic love arrived with the singer, the minstrel, who traveled from court to court, from castle to castle, relaying messages of love, concocting notions of love, torrents of poetic emotion, and in the courts men and women listened to these plaints and added more, their own. The singer heard new woes and put them into song, fostering a way to woo, but why did the minstrel sing in the first place, and what did traveling from one place to another do to produce songs of love? And later, did the printing press change love? Did the novel, offspring of Gutenberg's invention, transform love? Did love become an extended narrative with greater expectations, not a song but an opera?

> "When people used to learn about sex and die at thirty-five, they were obviously going to have fewer problems than people today who learn about sex at eight or so, I guess, and live to be eighty. That's a long time to play around with the same concept. The same boring concept." (Andy Warhol)

Dearest,

I don't think I've ever felt this way before, not exactly. Not like this. Is it possible? I thought about you all day, and then in the night too, and I felt I was going to die, because my heart was beating so fast, as if it were a wild bird caged in my chest, flapping its wings madly, trying to escape. Even if my heart were a wild bird, it would fly to you.

Paige wondered if love disinvented, too, undid her and him. She moved from the computer, which seemed now to glower, into the kitchen and walked to the sink and turned on the cold water. She watched the water flow into the teakettle, and then she put the kettle on the stove.

Dearest,

I love you especially when you're far away. I can feel you most when I don't see you. I carry you with me because your words carry, they fly, and yet they stay with me, stay close to me, the way you do even when you're not beside me. To be honest, love, sometimes words are all I need, words satisfy, your words, your words.

"Does that goddess know the words/ that satisfy burning desire?"
(Puccini, Madama Butterfly)

"I can love the other only in the passion of this aphorism."
(Jacques Derrida)

Paige thought writing might be an act of love, a kind of love affair, or a way of loving. She hoped it was a possibility, because even more, more horribly and wretchedly, she knew that it was also an incessant demand for love, enfeebling and humiliating. Always wanting, writing exposed its own neediness, like unrequited love, which might be the same thing, she wasn't sure. Except that when her own worthless desires rebuked her, her writing turned derisory, dissolved into worthlessness, and then became transparent.

> "My Love is of a birth as rare / As 'tis, for object, strange and high; / it was begotten by Despair / Upon Impossibility." (Andrew Marvell)

Dearest,

Maybe I'm always writing love, to you. That's the only way I can love you. What if love, like writing, was a rite enacted and re-enacted, or a habit, or a disguise to cloak a vacant lot near the streetcar named desire. Sometimes I think it would be better to remain silent, to let emptiness, vacancy, and loss have its full, dead weight, and that it would be better to let love and writing go, but, love, I don't want to stop writing or loving you.

It was nearly night. Paige visited old haunts without going anywhere, and she wallowed in dead loves and called upon memory, which competed with history, dividing her attention. Paige indulged herself, as if eating rich chocolates filled with her romantic past, and looked at pictures of former lovers stuck between pages in journals and albums. She mused and cut hearts out of paper towels, she held up one, then another, to the light. The hearts were large and ungainly, imperfect shapes meant to represent a romance or two or four. What would she write on a cheap paper heart?

> "I wrote you in a cave, the cave had no light, I wrote on pale blue paper, the words had no weight, they drifted and danced away before my eyes.

I couldn't give them substance. I could not make them bear down. I keep failing at this poetry, this game of love."

"O love is the crooked thing/ There is nobody wise enough/ To find out all that is in it..." (W. B. Yeats)

Dearest,

I know you think I have no perspective, and I know without perspective, everything is flat. Our love exists on available surfaces, beds, floors, on tabletops, on roofs. Tell me to stop. I can't help it, I want more, I want everything now. I love you, silently and stealthily. I love you as you have never been loved. I love you because I cannot love you.

"True hearts have ears and eyes, no tongues to speak; / They hear and see, and sigh, and then they break." (Sir Edward Dyer)

I love you.

It was just a sentence. Paige was struck by it and, she thought, stuck with it. Three ordinary, extraordinary, diminutive words, I love you, and just eight sweet letters. "O" repeats, oh yes. So little does so much, three little words, three little piggies make a sentence: I love you. The love sentence, arret d'amour.

Dearest,

What if I were sent to love you? What if I were the sentence "I love you"? Do you or I ever think of love as a sentence? I don't think so, you and I can't

stop to do that, we don't bother with its syntax, or who is sentenced, and for
how long. I think you and I can't think love at all. I can't now.

"What voice descends from heaven/to speak to me of love?"
(Verdi, Don Carlos)

"Wild thing, you make my heart sing./ You make everything, groovy./
Wild thing, I think I love you./ But I want to know for sure. Come on
and hold me tight. I love you." (The Troggs)

Feeling stupid, Paige tore up one of the hearts. She crumpled the others and looked at the mess. With hardly a second thought, she took
each newly crumpled heart and straightened it out, then patted down
all of the hearts until they were more or less flat and unwrinkled, and
lined them up on the table in front of her like a place mat. Paige smiled
at the hearts, paltry emblems of couplings gone. She even liked the
hearts better with creases, because she liked her lovers to have lines
around their mouths and eyes. So strange to concoct emblems, to
want signifiers of old loves, but it was, she thought, stranger not to
keep faith with memory and to desire, as obsessively, to forget.

Dearest,

I love you trembles inside me. It trembles and I can feel it just the way
I can feel you. You can't think love, I know you can't, not when you think
about me. I'm the one who loves you, no matter what, and I love you, no
matter that I want to take apart "I love you."

"But, untranslatable,/ Love remains/ A future in brains." (Laura Riding)

I love you.

What or who is the subject of this sentence, the object or the subject? Love confuses by constructing a subject/object relation that forgets what or why it is—who subject, who object. "You" never refuse "I," my love.

To Paige, a torn-up heart, its pieces scattered on the table top, represented all the broken hearts, not just hers. There were too many to name and count, countless numbers.

> "My first broken heart wasn't a romance. My heart broke before I even thought about love. It broke when I wanted something and couldn't have it, and I don't even remember when or what that was."

> "…When the original object of an instinctual desire becomes lost in consequence of repression, it is often replaced by an endless series of substitute objects, none of which ever give full satisfaction." (Freud)

Paige worried that memory, like love, was something she couldn't make decisions about, even when she made sense of the past, or it made some sense to her. Unlike love, memory was constant, and she was never without it. It was holding her hand as she tailored hearts.

Dearest,

I can't think straight, I can't do what I'm supposed to do. I can't eat or write or wash or cry or scream or die or decide, since loving you. Now "I love you" becomes a suffocated gasp, an involuntary gush. When you touch me,

I can't swallow, when you touch me, everything's a movie, and everything in me moves over to sigh. I gasp, I suffocate, I gush for you. If "I love you" becomes a lament, then I will gag on love and die.

"Know you not the goddess of love/ and the power of her magic?" (Wagner, Tristan and Isolde)

" 'Cause love comes in spurts/In dangerous flirts/and it murders your heart/They didn't tell you that part/Love comes in spurts/Sometimes it hurts/Love comes in spurts/oh no, it hurts." (Richard Hell)

I love you is the structure through which I love you. "I" is such a lonely, defiant letter. In this fatal and fateful sentence it's the first word—in the beginning, there was I—a pronoun, the nominal subject. In the love sentence, "I" submits to "you." That I is mine. That I is yours. That I is for you.

Dearest,

I'm the one who loves you better, longer, stronger, whose passion robs you of passion, whose daring steals your courage, whose boldness provokes your fear, whose gentleness savages you, whose absence electrifies you.

Paige waved a paper heart in the air and pretended to enact an ancient, time-honored ritual. She considered burning the heart in a funeral pyre and laughed out loud, a hollow sound with reverberations only for her. You never see yourself laughing, Paige realized. Once upon a time a man she loved caught her looking at herself in a mirror and noticed something she didn't want him to see.

"I'll be your mirror/ I'll be your mirror/ Reflect what you are/ In case you don't know." (Lou Reed)

"The woman who sang those lines died in a bicycle accident on an island. When she first sang the song, she was beautiful and somber and lonely, but not alone. She died in what's called a freak accident, and, at the time of her death, her body was swollen from years of shooting heroin, so she was no longer beautiful, but she was always, or still, lonely. It was spring when she died, it may have been summer."

I love you.

Love, the second word in the sentence, is the verb and acts by joining the two pronouns, pro-lovers, you and I. Love melts "you" into "I" or is it just grammar that bends "I" into "you," just that old subject to object-of-the-verb magic? Love dissolves disbelief, since it defies credulity. Love establishes an impossible, enduring, tender, spidery bridge between us, two poor pronouns. You and I are simple, one-syllable words, you and I need love.

"We do not see what we love, but we love in the hope of confirming the illusion that we are indeed seeing anything at all." (Paul de Man)

"Stereotype/Monotype/Blood type/Are you my type?" (Vernon Reid)

Paige shuffled the hearts and named each of them, and while she did, forced herself to remember him and herself with as much detail and vividness as she could bear. It's often hard to bear your own history.

A languid heaviness coursed through her and then settled like a stone in her stomach.

"I walked across the Brooklyn Bridge with him. The cars and trucks rumbling and tearing beneath us were terrifying. He thought it was weird that I didn't find any security in the fact that there was something solid under our feet. He held my hand, the way I hold this heart. Later, we went for Indian food. It was the first time I ever ate it. Then we went back to my place and made love for the first time, too. He stroked the insides of my thighs."

"Love u more than I did when u were mine." (Prince)

"The heart you betrayed,/ the heart you lost,/ see in this hour/ what a heart it was." (Bellini, Norma)

Dearest,

I'm afraid now too, though I'm not actually walking over a bridge. There isn't anything beneath my feet. I can't breathe or yawn or laugh or smile or cook or move or run or jump or stand or sit. I am restless. Bedeviled angel, sweet oxymoron, I ask questions you can't possibly answer. I'm not reasonable, absolutely not, why should I be, why should you? Really, I only have questions and you are a question to me, you are the question. I ask myself—you—what is it you want and what is it I want. Our wanting isn't going to be enough, though it is for now, wanting you is enough now. I can't live without you. See how you have destroyed me?

"For love—I would/ split open your head and put/ a candle in/ behind the eyes." (Robert Creeley)

Even so, or even more, I love you.

"You" is, you are, the last word, the last word and the first one too. In "you" there are two letters more than "I"—the difference is a diphthong, two vowels to create one sound—ooh, you-ooh. The vowels demand each other, they nestle together to make their sound.

Dearest,

My love clings to you. It is silent and dark, hidden from everyone else but you. Love is silent, sex is noisy. To write love, that's what I really want, and to write it to you must be finding silence also. Soundlessly, I'd put everything into words, and though the words are not actually love but how love would speak if it could—if my heart could talk—the words would make no sound. Yet, through my desire, with my will, they would strike a chord inside you. My words would creep and slither into you, if I had my way, and I want my way with you, and words once inert on paper would suddenly wing through the air like missiles. Silly or profound, they would fly into you, and you would embrace them or, more perfectly, they would embrace you. You would be entered, love, you would be my precious entrance to love and also my final destination, eternal enchantment.

"What is the use of speech? Silence were fitter:/ Lest we should still be wishing things unsaid./ Though all the words we ever spake were bitter,/ Shall I reproach you dead?" (Paul Verlaine)

Paige drank green tea and wondered what had happened to him, the lanky, green-eyed young man who hated himself, who said, I don't know why you like me. She hadn't liked him but had loved something about him.

"He was living on West Fourth Street and had been suicidal for years. He told everybody his brother was a movie star, and that was true. His room was in the back of a store and on the floor was a single mattress. The mattress looked like an unopened envelope. He said he had not made love in three years, and after he came, he cried, and the next day he hovered in a doorway, there was a violet gash on his neck. Then he disappeared forever."

Obliviously, I love you.

She was becoming stiff and rose from the table, and walked from room to room, imagining she was a ferocious animal. Paige paced back and forth, back and forth, not sleek as a tiger or cunning as a fox but on the prowl. She felt a little hungry.

"Even today love, too, is in essence as animal as it ever was." (Freud)

Paige took up the scissors again. Love, she considered with affection, should be generous, at the very least it should appear to be. She smiled absentmindedly as she cut more hearts, attempting to keep them attached like a chain of paper dolls. Was she fashioning love? Wasn't the memory better than the love? The shapes grew progressively more uneven and awkward.

"You planted yourself in my garden, taking up room, then, oh, you grew, you became a weed, you were so tall, with such nerve. Your satin trousers and you were much too sleek. I tried to escape, but you insisted. You kept on insisting, about what, toward what end, I can't remember. I wish flowers had never been looked at before. When we stood up, I felt taller, as tall as you, no, taller. You were awkward, but I remember all your questions."

Awkwardly, I love you.

Dearest,

I can still say it, common as it is, common as mud and as thick and undecipherable. In my dreams I cleave to you, I hold you, your body bent to mine, your body reminding me of someone else who is no longer here to love me, but then that's love, one body replaces another. I don't mean that, not just any other, yours, only you. And only you understand me, the me who loves you. You and I make meaning together, that's how love is, what love is—meaning. Meaning I love you. Meaning, I love you. "I love you" means I won't listen to reason.

> "Everybody has a different idea of love. One girl I knew said, 'I knew he loved me when he didn't come in my mouth.'" (Andy Warhol)

Paige thought about coloring the hearts and affixing titles to them. I'm glad no one can see me, she thought, and hummed aloud: I'm a little teapot, lift me up, pour me out. I'm a common heart, a commoner, a common metaphor, a cup of tea, a loaf of bread, a bouquet of posies. I am also beside myself. Hush, Paige admonished, be still, useless heart. Then she uncorked a bottle of red wine.

Commonly, I love you.

Since childhood, Paige had read poets and listened to the music of composers and songwriters who ordinarily took love as their subject. It made sense because love is mute, nearly unspeakable, so it needs a voice; still, it's impossible to give it fully or sufficiently. So, no one can say enough about love or for it, and it cannot be encompassed or conquered, since it's abstract, constantly inconsistent, outrageously ineffable, obdurate, and evasive. Therefore, Love endures as a subject worth taking up.

Paige allowed these sentiments and others entry, yet feared that whatever she had experienced and read, the cautionary tales she imbibed, couldn't protect her. She hoped, desperately, to invest in knowledge and gain strength for the lovesick nights, for those raw, endless hours that robbed her blind and stole her reason.

"The night murmurs/Its thousand loves/ And false counsels/ To soften and seduce the heart." (Puccini, Tosca)

"There was a time when I believed your love belonged to me/ Now I find that you're shackled to a memory/... How can I free your doubtful mind?/ And melt your cold, cold heart." (Hank Williams)

Blindly, I love you.

Dearest,

Even when my eyes hurt and everything's blurred, I keep writing and reading. Weak eyes still love stories. Remember when you said I'm full of stories. You are too. Isn't this how you seduced me? Wasn't it your story, how you told it, how I sank into it, submitted, and collapsed into the superb rendition of your life—into you? I thought I saw you in your story. And isn't this how I seduced you? It wasn't my beauty, was it? It wasn't my youth, was it? I think it was my story, one word after another after another, circling around you, gathering you to me. My lines roped you in, the way yours did me, our lines -- to continue this pathetic figure of speech—tangled, and we became one story. I have a French friend who always said about her love affairs, I'm having a little story with him. With words like sticky plums, I drew you close.

My grip, on you, on my own tales, is sometimes tenuous. I might slip, but I always love you.

Paige drank the wine, but she barely tasted it, she was transfixed. In her red bathrobe she looked comical, like a giant valentine. From time to time she glanced at the clock on the wall, but she wasn't sure what time it was. Every month the clock needed a new battery, but she forgot to change it. It was good that actual hearts didn't have batteries to be changed or recharged. Except there were pacemakers. Maybe that's why she felt run down, her heart was mimicking a machine. Paige stacked the paper hearts like honeyed pancakes.

Sweetly, I love you.

"She was so much in love, she wanted to make love all the time. He was away. She left their house and walked to a canal and saw a man standing on a bridge. She liked him, and it was easy to make love. Her exciting, grand passion threatened to make negligible any differences between one man and another. And, also, her love made her expansive, bigger than she was. She abandoned herself to the threat of self-annihilation—that's what love is—and spent the afternoon with the stranger. There was no restraint, she gave him everything he wanted, without regret. He gave her his address, and she tore it up later."

"Such wayward ways hath Love, that most part in discord/ Our wills do stand, whereby our hearts seldom do accord." (Henry Howard, Earl of Surrey)

Discordantly, I love you.

You are everything. "You" is everything to the sentence, I love you, for without "you," could "I" love?

Dearest,

It's strange to write "I love you." I don't mean to you, what's strange is to write it, to commit it to paper or the screen. I don't mean that it could be anyone but you when I write, I love you. Only you could be the you that I love. That's obvious. Isn't it obvious that I love you, and that, without you, I cannot love. You alone will see where I'm leading, where my thought carries me, because my thought carries me to you.

"The air is fragrant and oddly pure this morning. It wafts into my room and reminds me of days when I played for hours in the forest down the road, our jungle, or maybe it was next to the house then, back then. I can't remember. I remember how in the winter the pond would freeze over and all of us kids would ice skate, our hands tucked into our sleeves or sheltered safely in woolen mittens. Mittens are for little creatures who need shelter all the time. With mittens we are small animals with paws. The boys I played with—were you one of them? Even then? Steve, Ronnie, Jerry. They were always around the house. Jerry was dark and round. Ronnie, tall and blond, angular and angry, a bad boy. He became a lawyer. Steve stood apart and sulked. I wonder what happened to him."

Abruptly Paige jumped up from the table. At the sink she poured out the dregs of the tea. It was late, and the city was quiet, sleeping. Does a city sleep when it can't close its eyes? Isn't everyone wrong about something like love?

   Above her, in the upstairs apartment, a man strode heavily across the floor, from the refrigerator to the toilet, to the bed or in a different order. He stomped around like an enraged elephant, like a lover floundering from betrayal.

   Love is not silent, love is loud and violent and vicious with a love-ly, unsatisfactory language entangled on a wet tongue that entices. Paige danced around the kitchen, one hand gently patting her stomach.

   "I danced on 'Shop Around'/ but never the flip side/ 'Who's Lovin' You'/ boppin' was safer than grindin'/ (which is why you should not come around)" (Thulani Davis)

The language of and for love explains and isn't explanatory enough. If it's not learned well or early, but if one is a quick study, one could, with diligence, pick it up later. Paige wondered: Is psychoanalysis the way to learn to love later?

"The analyst's couch is the only place where the social contract explicitly authorizes a search for love—albeit a private one." (Julia Kristeva)

Childishly, I love you.

Dearest,

I don't want to love you badly. It's intangible, I suppose, how to love, but since it resides in language and the language of the body—can touch be taught?—it has a presence and effects, and it also exists with words. Love is a grammar, a style, replete with physical gestures and utterances and yellow marks flashing on gray-green computer screens. What if my hard drive crashes? What if you stop loving me? What if I stop loving you? What then? What words would ever be enough?

"...Once you see emotions from a certain angle, you can never think of them as real again. That's what more or less has happened to me. I don't really know if I was ever capable of love, but after the 60s, I never thought in terms of 'love' again." (Andy Warhol)

Dearest,

I hate this something you and I didn't name. It's gone out of control. With time, with time weighing us down, with no time to think about the future, with every fear about time passing—when will love come?—we grab love and hold it tight. Now we have it, now we have it, here it is, do you see it? I give it to you. I will forget everything else to love you.

"Let us forget the whole world!/ For you alone, dearest, I long!/ I have a past no more,/ I do not think of the future." (Verdi, Don Carlos)

"Love is begot by fancy, bred by ignorance, by expectation fed,
Destroyed by knowledge, and, at best,/Lost in the moment 'tis
possessed." (George Granville, Baron Lansdowne)

Impossibly, I love you.

"Love incapacitates me, my language is never enough. The language
is the matter, language is matter, it matters, it doesn't matter, we mat-
ter, we are matter, you and I are the matter, the matter of love, the stuff
of it, you and I. We are not enough, neither is love, there's no sense to
it, it doesn't make sense to you or me that this is what we are in, love,
a state of temporary grace with each other. It doesn't make sense, it's
not sound. It is a sound. It's your voice."

Dearest,

*You wanted to know, when you phoned (I love the sound of your voice)
what was on my mind. Just as you called I was thinking (I had pushed you
out of my mind in order to think), Some days it doesn't pay to get out of bed.
Then the telephone rang. Anyway it's Sunday, and I was thinking of Lewis
Carroll and Edith Wharton, who wrote in bed, enviable position, with a
board on her lap, traveling or at home, every morning. As she finished a
page, she let it drop to the floor, to be scooped up later by her secretary who
typed it. Lewis Carroll (I don't know where he wrote) and Wharton, it was
something about her love letters to Morton Fullerton, and Carroll's love of
Alice, his desire for young girls. Was his sense of the absurd best exemplified
by the ludicrous position he fell into, his love for such a small being. How
crazy it must have felt to him, spending Sundays with Alice, bending down
to hear her speak all day long, looming over the tiny object of his illicit af-*

fections. Even stranger to him must have been his wild, prohibited longing, if he actually felt it, to insert his penis into that girl's vagina. He must have felt so small and so big, and there it was, the topsy-turviness of his intimate world which he then concocted into words, and with words published (in the old sense), though no one knew, or wrote his body, I think, and its occupying desires. Alice had to become small to become big. Carroll had no sense of scale, did he, no proportion? Did he ever tell Alice, I love you? Did Lewis Carroll love Alice the way I love you or very differently? Is love the same for everyone, from its beginning to its end? If I wrote to you the way Wharton wrote her lover, would you like it? Please tell me, I want to give you what you want, I want to be everything you want me to be.

Now I'm crimson. I don't want to feel like this, but I can't help it, my words stall on my tongue, they won't come, and then they can't stop coming.

> "I'm so afraid that the treasures I long to unpack for you, that have come to me in magic ships from enchanted islands, are only, to you, the old familiar red calico & beads of the clever trader....Well! and if you do? It's your loss, after all!" (Edith Wharton, to Morton Fullerton)

Alone with longing, Paige verged toward alienation, like a spectator in her own amorous theater, where she could no longer play the ingenue. Now the paper hearts were actors, and some had important roles and others minor parts, just a line or two appended to a sexy action. Some characters were walk-ons, others appeared as comic relief.

Still, Paige fell in love, and, when she fell, plummeted into a lavish set of conventions. The modes were intractable and not her own, yet sensation maintained that her love was unique. Paige was capable of holding contradictory ideas and emotions, and, as ridiculous as it all was, she bore the irony. People bore it all the time, and some were so experienced in love's disappointments, they had discarded or discredited it. But Paige couldn't let it go, and, for its part, love wouldn't leave her alone.

Mother, I cannot mind my wheel;/My fingers ache, my lips are dry;/ Oh! if you felt the pain I feel!/But oh, who ever felt as I!" (Sappho)

Ironically, I love you.

Dearest,

Your love proposes and then marries me to a different idea of me, a new identity with its own poetic license, so now I'm different from myself but joined with your self, and you are different from yourself, at least from the way you have been, and the way your life has gone, and our love is the best difference that you and I will ever experience. Isn't it? Won't our love mark, cloud, inflect, protect, deform, consume, and subsume us? Won't it cast shadow or sunlight over all other experience? Isn't love the limit? Or, more gravely, like death, an inconsiderate end parenthesis.

"Do you not hear a voice in your heart/ which promises eternal happiness?" (Bellini, Norma)

"Who needs a heart when a heart can be broken?" (Terry Britten/ Graham Lyle)

Paige knocked her leg hard against the table. It hurt. Then a voice whispered: I don't want to die. Paige swung around in her chair, her solitude broken by a strange visitor, the voice an interruption or maybe a discovery, a sensation inside her. But nothing shakes or reaches the vicissitudes of the imaginary inside. I don't want to die, it repeated. She wasn't sure if it actually spoke, it was barely a voice, but she believed she'd heard it before.

Immortally, I love you.

"She wanted to be saved. She wanted to tear his eyes out. She wanted to eat his flesh. She wanted to carve her name on his forehead. She wanted him dead. She wanted him around. She wanted him to stand like a statue. She wanted him never to be sad. She wanted him to do what she wanted. She wanted him invulnerable and invincible. She wanted to look at him. She wanted him to get lost. She wanted to find him. She wanted him to do everything to her. She wanted to look at him.

"She had no idea who he was or what he was thinking. She only pretended that she knew him. He was an enigma of the present, the palpable unknown. He was the loved one, and he wasn't listening to reason. He would save her, and she would never die.

"She didn't want to die. She wanted to be saved."

Irrationally, I love you.

Paige turned off the computer. "She wanted to be saved" winked one last time. She tore up all the hearts and threw them in the garbage and, days later, wondered if they should have been recycled with the newspapers. She liked recycling.

> "...For the transaction between a writer and the spirit of the age is one of infinite delicacy, and upon a nice arrangement between the two the whole fortune of his works depend. Orlando had so ordered it that she was in an extremely happy position; she need neither fight her age, nor submit to it; she was of it, yet remained herself. Now, therefore, she could write, and write she did." (Virginia Woolf)

She sorted through some papers, closed her books, drew the covers off her bed, and undressed. She laid her head on a pillow and shut her eyes. Paige dismissed the present, and then the dead sat on a chair and talked, and love and hate gamboled, trading blows and kisses. Friends and enemies mingling, and her neck out of joint, Paige awoke just before the sun did. She rubbed sleep from her eyes and turned on the computer.

"Love is a necklace around the throat, it needs a durable clasp, so it can be put on and taken off again and again. Some necklaces you never want to take off, though."

Paige Turner is writing to you.

I love you.

Impressions of an Artist, with Haiku
A Portrait of Peter Dreher

A man, whose insufficient portrait will be rendered here, does not keep cats or wear a beard. He is of medium size, reasonable weight, and looks like an architect or a philosopher or an accountant. But he's an artist, has a studio and a house and travels between those places, and others, moving with deliberation, and going and coming.

This man likes stillness, so a cat might be a great companion, since nothing can be more still than a cat, especially when it hunts, except for an inanimate coffee cup or a corpse. Holding still for a long time suggests death and maybe infinity.

See. observation
Reclaims exhausted routines.
Noise can be music.

Understanding endlessness might make this artist, who is usually not the subject of a picture, capable of envisioning the scientific here-after. A very few minds can grasp the concept, the capacity for which might be compared with comprehending the finality of death, which few can, also, though death has an absolute place in life, creating the desire for immortality and, from that, as well as sexual curios-ity, everything else emerges: collecting antiques or jewelry or baseball cards, writing love poems, keeping busy, watching soccer, losing oneself in drink.

This man has typical worries, plumbing that goes wrong, the wrong comment at a party, a wronged lover, and he has some that are atypical, unless one is an artist and considers, daily, what is being portrayed or represented, a practice of and in pictures. He might ask himself, what is good about what I'm making? And never know. No one can know. But let's say of this artist that he is sincere; he would like to make honest paintings. What that is, he also acknowledges, vexes art-makers. No right way, no theological answers.

Cave drawings in Lescaux described prehistorical life, their travails, activities, triumphs. Early humans named their surroundings, and marked out days and nights in pictograms. They required records of their existence, since death—or whatever they called that event—savaged them, a monster swooping down and taking their breath away. Their sincerity has never been doubted. Is insincerity, he asks himself, laughing a little, the fault-line of so-called advanced civilization?

Owls, moonlight unmoors
Wolves, frantic prey scurry
Night licks voraciously.

The artist happened to be walking near a nighttime forest, musing about cave dwellers and their drawings, when he looked up and saw a star streak across the sky. Cave people saw shooting stars too, linking him to Neanderthals in a great chain of being and nonbeing, doing and undoing. But the exuberant flash might vex another man, on the other side of the world, who, watching it leap in his evening sky, could feel overwhelmed by the expanding universe and his own shortcomings. Then the artist imagined the distraught stranger weeping, and the other's sadness cast itself, like a ghost, across him and the heavens.

A star lives and dies, there is the wonder of it and the immensity of experience, good and bad. Is there an antonym for "wonder"? Hell. Mystery's opposite? Boredom. By now he was in his studio, staring at a water glass. He had looked at it for more than thirty years, the very same glass. Some people thought he was crazy. But he was only beginning to see it, or he kept seeing it differently and he tried to depict that, how it changed, how his capacity changed, and he himself changed over the years. He didn't mean to paint an autobiography, but he was, also.

The next day, he placed a skull on a black cloth. It considered him, uncannily. "Alas, poor Yorick," the artist repeated aloud several times. The skull seemed to levitate. Other than death, outcomes and results were unpredictable, in any case he wouldn't want to predict the end, unless he could begin again, immediately. The point, perhaps, was to find what he was looking for through its execution; he himself had not lost anything specific, or everything was lost and found again in endless repetitions, and, the more he worked, the more change he discovered in minute variations. He might be surprised by the color of an eggplant or the verve of a flower or the eerie acoustic of an empty room.

A phantasm or a wisp of conversation lay beneath the surface, a palimpsest, rising, later, onto the surface as a still life. In practice, the reality of imperfection and the hope for perfection strafed his imagination and capabilities; he was similar to, and dissimilar from, others in trying and sometimes giving up. Friction between styles and forms required conscious choices, approaches and adaptations to changing conditions in need of living concepts. Things made in time, of time, he thought.

A green vase, a blue
Vase on a dark wood table,
Images inside cups.

The artist worked in solitude which brought him a kind of happiness, but even in solitude, in a peaceful place, the soot of mixed emotions collected in corners. A recollection absorbed him, he glanced at the garden, and an image passed like a summer's day. His father sent to the Russian front, never to return, his mother whispering to him, consolingly; then he thought he heard her voice, but it was only a breeze whipping through the bamboo. She found him curious, amusing, and perhaps as a consequence—though he could never know—he was rarely lonely.

A farmer's cheese, green tea tickling his tongue, a long letter from a friend, a sweet kiss when he needed it, the sun's regular rise, at slightly different times, during which he might be aroused by an idea, these contented him. He also swayed on shaky foundations, balancing as best he could, unbalanced by what no one can control.

Drawing with pencil.
Sketch a paradise. Damned
War, never again.

Be aware, he remonstrated with himself, otherwise time passes with only a sense of its absence, the way that distraught man, on the other side of the world, might feel it. He buttoned his shirt and combed his hair. He might have a cup of tea, eat a biscuit, sit in a chair, listen to Bach, or watch TV. Half-empty or half-full? His friends joked with him. Invisible choruses sang dissonant arias about the arbitrariness of choice and the dissipations of history, the news on TV shattered composure, as it if were a pane of glass. The common libretto was comic and tragic, everyone's opera.

Not true, not false, not one, not the other. Standing before an object, his job was to see it, as it was to him, simple and complex.

Repetition with variation: A man, whose insufficient portrait has been rendered just now, does not keep cats or sport a beard. He is of medium size, sensible weight, and could appear to be an academic or a violinist or a bookseller. He's a painter, has a studio in a village and a house near a city, and journeys between those places, and others, coming and going, thoughtfully, deliberately.

Day by day, he would add, every day is a good day.

Madame Realism's Conscience

"Whatever it is, I'm against it."
—Groucho Marx, Horse Feathers

Way past adolescence, Madame Realism's teenaged fantasies survived, thought bubbles in which she talked with Hadrian about the construction of his miraculous wall or Mary Queen of Scots right before the Catholic queen was beheaded. Madame Realism occasionally fronted a band or conversed with a president, for instance, Bill Clinton, who appeared to deny no one an audience. Could she have influenced him to change his course of action or point of view? Even in fantasy, that rarely happened. She persevered, though. At a state dinner thought bubble, Madame Realism whispered to Laura Bush, "Tell him not to be stubborn. Pride goeth before a fall." Laura looked into the distance and nodded absent-mindedly.

Over the years, Madame Realism had heard many presidential rumors, some of which were confirmed by historians: Eisenhower had a mistress; Mamie was a drunk; Lincoln suffered from melancholia; Mary Lincoln attended séances; Roosevelt's mistress, not Eleanor, was by his side when he died; Eleanor was a lesbian; Kennedy, a satyr; Jimmy Carter, arrogant; Nancy Reagan made sure that Ronnie, after being shot, took daily naps. When Betty Ford went public with her addictions and breast cancer, she became a hero, but Gerald

Ford will be remembered primarily for what he didn't do or say. He didn't put Nixon on trial; and, he denied even a whiff of pressure on him to pardon the disgraced president. Ford's secrets have died with him, but maybe Betty knows.

> The Pope, President Clinton, Henry Kissinger, and an Eagle Scout were on a plane, and it was losing altitude, about to crash. But there were only three parachutes. President Clinton said, "I'm the most powerful leader in the Free World. I have to live," and he took a parachute and jumped out. Henry Kissinger said, "I'm the smartest man in the world. I have to live," and he jumped out. The Pope said, "Dear boy, please take the last parachute, I'm an old man." The Eagle Scout said, "Don't worry, there are two left. The smartest man in the world jumped out with my backpack."

Whatever power was, it steamrolled behind the scenes and kept to its own rarefied company, since overexposure vitiated its effects. So, when a president came to town, on a precious visit, people wanted to hear and see him, but they also wanted to be near him. They stretched out their arms and thrust their bodies forward, elbowing their way through the crush for a nod or smile; they waved books in front of him for his autograph, dangled their babies for a kiss, and longed for a pat on the back or a handshake. Madame Realism had listened to people say they'd remember this moment for the rest of their days, the commander in chief, so charismatic and handsome. And, as fast as he had arrived, the president vanished, whisked away by the Secret Service, who surrounded him, until at the door of Air Force One, he turned, smiled, and waved to them one last time.

Without access to power's hidden manifestations, visibility is tantamount to reality, a possible explanation for the authority of images. Everyone comprised a kind of display case or cabinet of curiosities and became an independent, unbidden picture. Madame Realism dreaded this particular involuntarism; but interiority and subjectivity were invisible, they were not statements. Your carriage, clothes, weight, height, hairstyle, and expression told their story, and what you appeared to be was as much someone else's creation as yours.

You never get a second chance to make a first impression.

If the President of the United States—POTUS, to any West Wing devotee—dropped his guard, power itself shed a layer of skin. Ever cognizant of that, one of the great politicians of the twentieth century, Lyndon Baines Johnson, called out to visitors while he was on the toilet. Suddenly, Madame Realism took shape nearby, and seeing a visitor's embarrassment, she shouted to the president, "Hey, what's up with that?" LBJ laughed mischievously.

It gave her an idea: maybe he had consciously made himself the butt of the joke, before others could. A Beltway joke writer had once said that self-deprecating humor was essential for presidents, though Johnson's comic spin was extreme and made him into a bathroom joke. Presidential slips of the tongue, accidents and mishaps supposedly humanized the anointed, but the unwitting clowns still wielded power. Laughter was aimed at the mighty to level the playing field, but who chose the field? To her, the jokes also zeroed in on powerlessness; and Madame Realism trusted in their uneven and topsy-turvy honesty. To defame, derogate, offend, satirize, parody, or exaggerate was not to lie, because in humor's province, other truths govern.

"Any American who is prepared to run for president should automatically, by definition, be disqualified from ever doing so."
—Gore Vidal

She herself followed, whenever possible, G.K. Chesterton's adage: "For views I look out of the window, my opinions I keep to myself." But presidents were nothing if not opinions, and, at any moment, they had to give one. Maybe since they were kids, they had wished and vied for importance, to pronounce and pontificate, and they had to be right or they'd die. The public hoped for a strong, honest leader, but more and more it grew skeptical of buzz and hype, of obfuscation passing as answer, of politicians' lies. Yet who one called a liar conformed to party of choice.

> Some people are talking, and one of them says, "All Republicans are assholes."
> Another says, "Hey, I resent that!"
> First person says, "Why, are you a Republican?"
> Second person answers, "No, I'm an asshole!"

Some jokes were all-purpose, for any climate. Madame Realism first heard the asshole joke about lawyers, but most proper nouns would fit, from Democrats to plumbers, teachers to artists. Jokes could be indiscriminate about their subjects, since the only necessity was a good punchline that confronted expectation with surprise, puncturing belief, supposition, or image.

"Mr. Bush's popularity has taken some serious hits in recent months, but the new survey marks the first time that over fifty percent of respondents indicated that they wished the president was a figment of their imagination." —Andy Borowitz, The Borowitz Report

Her fantasies often skewered Madame Realism, threw her for a loop, but at times they fashioned her as the host of a late-night talk show, when, like Jon Stewart and Stephen Colbert, she held the best hand. Madame Realism imagined questioning presidential also-rans, who had sacrificed themselves on the altar of glory and ambition—Al Gore, John Kerry, the ghost of Adlai Stevenson. Suddenly Adlai stated, out of nowhere, "JFK never forgave me, you know, for not supporting him at the Democratic convention." Then a familiar, haunted look darkened his brown eyes, and pathos quickly soured their banter. Pathos didn't fly on late-night TV.

Anyone but an action hero understood that even a rational decision or intelligent tactic might awaken unforeseen forces equipped with their own anarchic armies, and some presidents agonized under mighty power's heft. In portraits of him, Abraham Lincoln morphed from eager Young Abe, saucy, wry candidate for Congress from Illinois, to a father overwhelmed with sadness at his young son's death, to a gravely depressed man, the president who took the nation to its only civil war. Madame Realism treasured soulful Abraham Lincoln, because he appeared available to her contemporary comprehension, a candidate ripe for psychoanalysis. She pictured speaking kindly to him, late at night, after Mary had gone to sleep, the White House dead and dark, when words streamed from him, and, as he talked about his early days, his ravaged face lit up, remembering life's promise.

What do you call Ann Coulter and Jerry Falwell in the front seat of a car? Two airbags.

In the nineteenth century, even Thomas Carlyle believed "all that a man does is physiognomical of him." A face revealed a person's character and disposition, and, if skilled in reading it, like physiognomists who were its natural science proponents, why human beings acted the way they did could be discerned. Also, their future behavior might be predicted. Criminals and the insane, especially, were analyzed, because the aberrant worried the normal, and, consequently, deranged minds had to be isolated from so-called sane ones. The sane felt crazy around the insane.

Though face-reading as a science had gone the way of believing the world was flat—poor Galileo!—facial expressions dominated human beings' reactions; each instinctively examined the other for evidence of treachery, doubt, love, fear, and anger. Defeat and success etched an ever-changing portrait of the aging face that, unlike Dorian Gray's, mutated in plain sight. Animals relied on their senses for survival, but beauty made all fools, democratically. And though it is constantly asserted that character is revealed by facial structure and skin, plastic surgery's triumphal march through society must designate new standards. For instance, Madame Realism asked herself, how do you immediately judge, on what basis, a person's character after five facelifts?

"Images are the brood of desire."
—George Eliot, Middlemarch

Before appearing on TV, politicians were commanded: Don't move around too much in your chair, don't be too animated, you'll look crazy, don't touch your face or hair, don't flail your arms, don't point your finger. Their handlers advised them: keep to your agenda, make your point, not theirs. The talking heads tried to maintain their pose and composure, but these anointed figures faltered in public, and, with the ubiquity of cameras, their every wink, smirk, awkwardness, or mistake was recorded and broadcast on the Internet, the worse the better.

At a political leadership forum led by his son, Jeb Bush, former President Bush wept when he spoke about Jeb losing the 1994 governorship of Florida. Madame Realism took a seat next to him after he returned to the table, still choked up. "Did you cry," she asked, "because you wish Jeb were president, not your namesake?" President Bush ignored her for the rest of the evening.

Why are presidents so short?
So senators can remember them.

A happy few were born to be poker-faced. A rare minority suffered from a disease called prosopagnosis, or face blindness; the Greek prosopon means face, and agnosia is the medical term for the loss of recognition. An impairment destroys the brain's ability to recognize faces, which usually happens after a trauma to it; but if the disease is developmental or genetic, and occurs before a person develops an awareness that faces can be differentiated, sufferers never know that it is ordinary to distinguish them. They see no noses, eyes, lips, but a blur, a cloudy, murky space above the neck. What is their life like?

Their world? How do they manage? But she couldn't embody their experience, not even in fantasy.

> He wants power
> He has power
> He wants more
> And his country will break in his hands,
> Is breaking now.
> —Alkaios, ca. 600 BC, from Pure Pagan, translated by Burton Raffel

Those who ran for president, presumably, hungered for power, to rule over others, like others might want sex, a Jaguar, or a baby. Winning drives winners, and maybe losers, too, Madame Realism considered. Power, that's what it's all about, everyone always remarked. But why did some want to lead armies and others want to lead a Girl Scout troop, or nothing much at all? With power, you get your way all the time.

She wanted her way, she knew she couldn't get it all the time, but how far would Madame Realism go to achieve her ends? She wasn't sure. And, why were her ends modest, compared, say, with Hadrian's? Like other children, she'd been trained not to be a sore loser, to share, not to hit, but probably Hadrian hadn't. And, what a joke, she laughed to herself, the power of toilet training.

> "Things are more like they are now than they ever were before."
> —Dwight D. Eisenhower

Thought bubbles gathered over her head, and she attempted, as if in a battle, to thrust into those airy-fairy daydreams fates that she didn't crave, like serving as a counselor in a drug clinic or checking microchips for flaws. In fantasy only, Madame Realism ruled her realm, and she could go anywhere, anytime. She would be lavished with awards for peace and physics and keep hundreds of thousands of stray animals on her vast properties. Fearlessly and boldly, she would poke holes in others' arguments, and sometimes she did influence a president. She did not imagine having coffee with the owner of the local laundromat, she didn't make beds or sweep floors. Though she believed she didn't care about having great power, her wishes, like jokes, claimed their own special truths.

"The King of Kings is also the Chief of Thieves. To whom may I complain?"—The Bauls

There was a story standup comic Mort Sahl told about JFK and him. Mort Sahl was flying on Air Force One with Kennedy, when they hit a patch of rough turbulence. JFK said to Sahl, "If this plane crashed, we would probably all be killed, wouldn't we?" Sahl answered, "Yes, Mr. President." Then JFK said, "And it occurs to me that your name would be in very small print." The comic was put in his place, power did that. Madame Realism wondered how wanting power or wanting to be near it was different, if it was. Maybe, she told herself, she would give up some of her fantasies and replace them with others. But could she?

Save Me from the Pious and the Vengeful
for Joe Wood 1965-1999

Out of nothing comes language and out of language comes nothing and everything. Everything challenges the tenuous world order. Every emotion derails every other one. One rut is disrupted by the emergence of another. I like red wine, but began drinking white, with a sudden thirst, and now demand it at 6 P.M. exactly, as if my life depended upon it. That was a while ago.

What does a life depend upon? And from whom do I beg forgiveness so quietly I'm never heard? With its remarkable colors and aftertastes, the wine, dry as wit, urges me to forgive myself. I try.

Life's aim, Freud thought, was death. I can't know this, but maybe it's death I want, since living comes with its own exigencies, like terror. In dreams, nothing dies, but birth can't be trusted, either. I remember terrible dreams and not just my own. Memory is what everyone talks about these days. Will we remember, and what will we remember, who will be written out, ignored, or obliterated. Someone could say: They never existed. It's a singular terror.

The names of the dead have to be repeated daily. To forget them has a meaning no one understands, but there comes a time when the fierce pain of their absence dulls and their voices become so faint they can't be heard.

And then what do the living mean by being alive, how dare we?

The year changes, the millennium, and from one day to the next, something must have been discarded, or neglected, something was abandoned, left to wither or ruin. You didn't decide to forget. People make lists, take vitamins, and they exercise. I bend over, over and over.

I'm not good at being a pawn of history.

The news reports that brain cells don't die. I never believed they did. The tenaciousness of memory, its viciousness really—witness the desire over history for revenge—has forever been a sign that the brain recovers. But it's unclear what it recovers.

Try to hang on to what you can. It's all really going. So am I. Someone else's biography seems like my life. I read it and confuse it with my own. I watch a movie, convinced it happened to me. I suppose it did happen to me. I don't know what I think anymore. I don't know what I don't think. I'm someone who tells things.

Once, I wanted to locate movie footage of tidal waves. They occurred in typical dreams. But an oceanographer told me that a tidal wave was a tsunami, it moved under the ocean and couldn't be seen. This bothered me for a long time. I wondered what it was that destroyed whole villages, just washed them away. In dreams, I'm forced to rescue myself. This morning's decision: let life rush over me. The recurring tidal wave is not about sexual thralldom, not the spectacular orgasm, not the threat of dissolution and loss of control through sex—that, too—but a wish to be overcome by life rather than to run it. To be overrun.

I don't believe any response, like invention, is sad. The world is made up of imagining. I imagine this, too. Things circle, all is flutter. Things fall down and rise up. Hope and remorse, beauty and viciousness, and imagination, wherever it doggedly hides, unveil petulant realities. I live in my mind, and I don't. There's scant privacy for bitterness or farting or the inexpressible; historically, there was an illusion of privacy. Illusions are necessary. The wretched inherit what no one wants.

What separates me from the world? Secret thoughts?

What Americans fear is the inability to have a world different from their fathers' and mothers'. That's why we move so much, to escape history.

Margaret Fuller said: I accept the universe. I try to embrace it. But I leave it to others to imagine the world in ways I can't.

I leave it to others.

Out of nothing comes language and out of language comes nothing and everything. I know there will be stories. Certainly, there will always be stories.

Publication History

"Chartreuse" in *Cabinet* 12 Fall/Winter 2003, Brooklyn, NY

"Give Us Some Dirt," in *Bald Ego*, Vol 1, #2, , Fall 2003,
New York, NY pp. 52-3

"The Original Impulse," in *Electric Literature* #6, Dec. 2010

"A Greek Story," in *Crowd*, Vol 7 # 1, ed. Samantha Hunt, Brooklyn NY,
Fall 2006, pp. 14-15.

"That's How Wrong My Love Is," in *The Happy Hypocrite: Hunting and
Gathering*, Issue 2, ed. Maria Fusco, fall 2008, Bookworks, London,
pp. 49-52.

"Playing Hurt," in *Conjunctions* #47, Bard College, Annandale on
Hudson, NY, 2006, pp. 341-5.

"Lunacies," in *Luna Luna in the Sky, Will you make me Laugh or Cry?* Ed.
Steven Hull, Nothingmoments Press, Los Angeles, 2009, pp. 109-111.

"The Way We Are," *Black Warrior Review*, Vol. 33 Num. 2, Spring/Summer
2007, University of Alabama, Tuscaloosa, pp. 127-9.

"Madame Realism's Conscience," *Mr. President* (catalogue), exhibition, The University Art Museum, The University at Albany, Spring 2007, pp. 7-13.

"Impressions of An Artist, with Haiku: A Portrait of Peter Dreher," in *PETER DREHER: Tag Um Tag Guter Tag (Every day is a good day)*, modo Verlag GmbH, Freiburg, 2008, pp. 54-55.

"Love Sentence" (novella), *American Imago*, 50-3, Fall 1993, pp. 255-275; revised and reprinted, LOVE SENTENCE (chapbook), drawings: Tami Demaree, design: Emily CM Anderson, Nothing Moments Press, 2007.

"More Sex," in *Black Clock*, ed. Steve Erickson, #7, fall 2007, California Institute of the Arts, 2 pages (unnumbered).

"Other Movies," *Binational* catalogue, Boston: ICA and Museum of Fine Art, October 1988; reprinted, in LIFE AS WE SHOW IT: Writing on Film, ed. Masha Tupitsyn and Brian Pera, San Francisco, City Lights Books, 2009, pp.13-22.

"A Simple Idea," in *The Literary Review*, ed. Rene Steinke, Spring 2002, Fairleigh Dickinson University, NJ, vol. 45, 3, pp. 453-6.

"Save Me from the Pious and the Vengeful," in *New York Writes After September 11*, ed. Ulrich Baer, New York University Press, New York and London, 2002, pp. 294-6; reprinted, in PEN America, "Fear Itself," issue # 10, ed. M. Mark, New York 2009, pp. 193-4.

"Letter" ("Letter to Ollie"), in *McSweeney's 8*, ed. Paul Maliszewski, New York, 2002, pp. 17-19.

"The Substitute," in *Strictly Casual*, ed. Amy Prior, Serpent's Tail, London, 2003, pp. .
"Later," in *Black Clock* 2, ed. Steve Erickson, published by California Institute of Art, Fall 2004, pp. 106-7.

"The Recipe," in *Orit Raff: Insatiable* (monograph), Daniella De-Nur-Publishers, Tel Aviv, Spring 2005, pp. 69-76; revised and reprinted,
"The Recipe," in This Is Not Chick Lit, ed. Elizabeth Merrick, Random House, NY, 2006, pp. 298-309.

"The Shadow of Doubt," in *Blur of the Otherworldly: Contemporary Art, Technology, and the Paranormal*, eds. Mark Alice Durant and Jane D. Marsching, in Cultural Theory 9, published by the Center for Art and Visual Culture, University of Maryland, Baltimore County, UMBC, 2006.

"But There's A Family Resemblance," in *Shoot the Family*, ed. Ralph Rugoff, ICI, New York, 2006, pp. 54-61.

"The Unconscious is Also Ridiculous," in *Black Clock* #12, ed. Steve Erickson, California Institute of the Arts, November 2010, 2 pages (unnumbered).

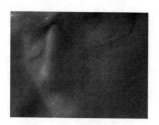

Lynne Tillman is the author of five novels, three collections of short stories, one collection of essays, and two other nonfiction books. She collaborates often with artists and writes regularly on culture, and her fiction is anthologized widely. Her last collection of short stories, *This Is Not It*, included twenty-three stories based on the work of twenty-two contemporary artists. Her novels include *American Genius, A Comedy* (2006), *No Lease on Life* (1998), which was a *New York Times* Notable Book of 1998 and a finalist for the National Book Critics Circle Award, *Cast in Doubt* (1992), *Motion Sickness* (1991), and *Haunted Houses* (1987). *The Broad Picture* (1997) collected Tillman's essays, which were published in literary and art periodicals. She is the fiction editor at *Fence* Magazine, professor and writer-in-residence in the Department of English at the University at Albany, and a recent recipient of a Guggenheim Fellowship.

Self by Lynne Tillman, using Blackberry

Dear Reader,

This is a Red Lemonade book, also available in all reasonably possible formats—limited artisan-produced editions, in trade paperback editions, and in all current digital editions, as well as online at the Red Lemonade publishing community: http://redlemona.de

A word about this community. Over my years in publishing, I learned that a publisher is the sum of all its constituent parts: yes and above all the writers, and yes, the staff, but also all the people who read our books, talk about our books, support our authors, and those who want to be one of our authors themselves.

So I started a company called Cursor, designed to make these constituent parts fit better together, into a proper community where, finally, we could be greater than the sum of the parts. The Red Lemonade publishing community is the first of these and there will be more to come—for the current roster of communities, see the Cursor website at http://thinkcursor.com.

For more on how to participate in the Red Lemonade publishing community, including the opportunity to share your thoughts about this book, read what others have to say about it, to learn more about Lynne Tillman and her novels all of which we now have back in print, as well as to share your own manuscripts with fellow writers, readers, and the Red Lemonade editors, go to the Red Lemonade website: http://redlemona.de.

Also, we want you to know that these sites aren't just for you to find out more about what we do, they're places where you can tell us what you do, what you want, and to tell us how we can help you. Only then can we really have a publishing community be greater than the sum of its parts.

Let me also note the following editorial credits. I edited and copy-edited this book with the assistance of Anne Horowitz. Daniel Schwartz proofread it.

Regards,
Richard Nash
Publisher